The Caribbean Endeavor

The Caribbean Endeavor

Larry Andrews

The Caribbean Endeavor

The novel is a work of fiction. Names, descriptions, entities, and incidents
included in the story are products of the author's imagination. Any resemblance to actual persons, events, and entities is entirely coincidental.

ISBN-13: 978-1547228553
ISBN-10: 1547228555

For my wife Sue, an avid traveler.

Acknowledgements

My wife Sue, for always being there.

My good friend, Captain John King, for maritime insights.

My grandson, Tyler Andreassen, for martial art acumen.

Eddy Bay, for initial manuscript editing.

Millie Ames Writer's Workshop, for the critique

during manuscript development.

CONTENTS

CHAPTER 1

The Assignment

He had been tracking her for months. It was twilight when he vaulted the fence and approached the estate where she was rumored to be. Advancing to the patio area behind the mansion, he saw her. He was amazed at her beauty. Tall and shapely, she stood on the other side of the pool, a vision of loveliness. Her long dark hair tumbled over her shoulders and her open dressing gown revealed that she had been swimming in the nude. From the shadows it appeared she was holding something in her hands. It was then that he noticed the moving crimson spot on his chest. She had a pistol pointed directly at him and was about to . . . . .

"Marcus, report!" The PA system boomed across the cubicles on the tenth floor of the CIA office complex in Manhattan, startling Marcus from his daydream. He could not get used to that call from his boss. *Why can't he use the phone and dial my extension? Why does he have to broadcast to the world that he wants to see me? What did I ever sign up for?* thought Marcus.

Recruited by the CIA in his senior year at NYU, he was becoming disillusioned with his first real job out of college. The recruiter had told him that poli-sci graduates were just what the CIA needed. They promised him it would be an exciting job and he would see the world. He naturally thought of James Bond. So far, reality had turned out to be far from the promise. Running background investigations on foreign delegates to the UN who were suspected of being anti-American was really pretty boring, he thought, certainly not worthy of his talents.

"Marcus, now!" boomed the PA system again. Marcus hurried out of his cubicle to his boss's office.

"Close the door and sit, Marcus," said his boss.

"Look, I know I am a little behind in the two investigations I was recently assigned, but . . . ," Marcus started to respond.

"Just relax, Marcus, and listen," interrupted the boss, waving his hand to get his attention.

"I know you have been a little unhappy with your assignments during the past six months. Even though they have been interrupted with agent training, they have probably seemed pretty boring. You should understand it is work that has to be done, but that's not why I called you in. Marcus, you are going on an operational assignment."

Marcus immediately perked up, saying, "Wow, I mean, yes, sir."

"We are sending you on a Caribbean cruise," continued the boss. "Franco Gambioni, the local Mafia crime boss, is taking his family on a cruise. You may not be aware but the FBI and we have been trying to get something on him for years, and we want to know what he is up to. The word on the street is there may be a connection with a drug cartel developing in Colombia. This most likely isn't just a family vacation. We suspect it's a setup for a meeting of the two factions to cement a deal. We want you to watch Franco and report back if a meeting occurs and who with."

"A real luxury cruise liner?" asked Marcus, as if he hadn't heard a word of his assignment and was still digesting his boss's initial words. His family taking the harbor cruise around Manhattan was the closest he had ever experienced being on a ship. He remembered his grandfather telling him about the crossing with his grandmother on a steamship from Sweden. As he recalled, it didn't sound that great. Small cabin, seasickness and bad food all made it sound like sailing was really not the greatest. Of course, the cruise liners of today are quite different and television ads make them appear quite luxurious. This could be the assignment of a lifetime. A 12-day cruise at the expense of the United States government. Cool!

"Marcus! Yes, the Golden Duchess of the Duchess Cruise Line. Were you listening to your assignment?" asked his boss. Not waiting for an answer, he continued, "Now we want you to assume a low profile on board and just watch the activities of the Gambioni family. Keep notes on who they associate with and any contacts they may make on shore excursions."

Marcus overcame his excitement and became very attentive as his boss went into detail about the Gambioni family and specific things he should watch for. The meeting lasted a good hour, covering not only his assignment but the travel details that would be arranged.

———•◦•———

After he graduated from college, Marcus had continued to live with his parents in what used to be the Scandinavian section of Brooklyn. However, three months before he had felt financially secure enough to get his own place. He had rented a small studio apartment on the upper east side of Manhattan. With the pleasurable thoughts of an ocean cruise still swimming in his head, he arrived home and, with the Murphy bed down, began laying out what he thought he should pack for the trip. Marcus really didn't have that many clothes. In fact, his entire wardrobe would fit very easily into the one small suitcase that one of his colleagues at the agency had loaned him. As he was closing the bag, the apartment doorbell rang and startled him.

Who could that be? he thought.

"Marcus, it's me. Jenna." Rapid pounding on the door followed. Marcus opened the door and there stood Jenna, one of his colleagues at the office.

"What are you doing here?" he asked.

With a huge smile and flashing eyes, Jenna responded, "Surprise, I am your new wife."

"What?"

"Yes, the agency feels you would be less conspicuous if we were a married couple on a honeymoon cruise. Don't worry; they've made all the arrangements. In fact I have our tickets here. We have a mini suite on the Golden Duchess. And it's on the deck directly above the two suites the Gambioni family has."

Noting the surprised and somewhat hesitant expression on Marcus's face, Jenna continued, "Now don't get too excited or concerned. Our suite is configured with separate beds and it will be no different than if you were traveling with your sister. The agency feels this will be good training for both of us for future missions either of us may be assigned to. Now I know you mentioned that you plan to stay at your folks' house over the weekend, and that they would take you to the cruise ship on Monday. Well, I have another surprise for you. We have a stipend to buy clothes for both of us. This came through after you left the office today and I see you already packed your bag. Well, it may have to be repacked as we're both going shopping . . ."

Jenna had also attended NYU and had been recruited by the CIA. Before joining the agency, they had had little contact. They may have been in some classes together, but Marcus couldn't remember. It really wasn't until they joined the agency that they became acquainted. Jenna was a plain Jane, a dishwater blonde who wore her hair long and straight. She seldom used makeup and her clothes were functionally plain. They both had been at the agency a year and a half and were commonly referred to as the young ones. There was certainly no physical attraction between them and they only communicated periodically when working on similar reports. Thus Marcus was totally surprised to find they had been teamed up together.

Now the thought of going shopping with her to buy clothes

for the trip really didn't seem too appealing. Before he could verbalize any complaints, "Chatty Cathy" Jenna changed the subject with a disturbing question. "Marcus, didn't you once say that you had a childhood friend that you thought worked for the Mafia?"

"Oh, my God, Sal," said Marcus. Salvatore Indelicato had been Marcus's childhood friend. Sal's father had a bakery in the business section of Brooklyn just a few blocks from Marcus's home. After school he would go to the bakery with Sal and help him clean the dough mixer, which was his assigned chore. It had to be done before he could go out to play. They had been very close friends all through grammar school and high school but lost touch after Marcus went to college. He heard that Sal had gone into the personal security business and later become a bodyguard for the mob.

"He could be working for the Gambioni family. That could be a disaster."

"Now don't panic." said Jenna, "We don't know that he does, and we don't know if he is going, if he does work for them."

Marcus continued to muse out loud, "I haven't seen him in years but I am sure we would recognize each other. He certainly would be surprised to see me on a cruise but I think he would buy the newlywed bit. I am sure he doesn't know I work for the CIA. In fact, only my mother and father know. We never told my sister; she just thinks I have an office job in Manhattan. This could get complicated."

The two-and-a-half story Peterson house in the middle of the block had a small stoop but a large bay window. This allowed for an excellent view up and down the street.

"Marcus, the limo is here," Marcus's dad called from the front room where he had been watching for its arrival.

Marcus came out of the kitchen where he was being peppered with questions and advice from his mother and sister about the trip. His father's call was a welcome break. The whole family went out the front door. The father carried Marcus's suitcase, while mother and sister said goodbyes and gave advice at the same time. All were totally surprised to see a stretch limo, complete with a strange young woman inside. It had already picked up Jenna, and Marcus almost didn't recognize her. He hadn't mentioned to his parents that he was teamed with Jenna or that they would be posing as a married couple. They were thus surprised to see her in the limo, but there was no time for explanations. Marcus's bag was loaded in the trunk. He gave a quick kiss to his mother and they were off.

"You clean up pretty good. I almost didn't recognize you. Your hair, makeup, and the dress, sure isn't the Jenna I thought I knew," Marcus said as they drove away.

"Thanks, Marcus, I am not sure whether that was a compliment or not but I'll take it as one. Look, when we arrive at the pier, they will take our bags directly to the ship. You did attach the baggage tag with our cabin number that I gave you?" Jenna asked, continuing with, "Do you have your passport?"

"Yes to all," replied Marcus.

"Give it here and when we arrive, just follow me," continued Jenna as she added it to a file folder she was carrying that contained all their travel documents. Arrival at the pier was as she predicted. After being relieved of their bags, they were directed into a large area where all were required to show their boarding passes, sign a medical disclaimer, and proceed to a long queue in front of the registration counter. Jenna, spotting a shorter line labeled "Preferred," said, "Quick, Marcus, follow me," as she quickly ushered Marcus into the shorter queue. Here they were relieved of their passports and boarding passes, presented with cruise cards and directed through security to a waiting area.

An elderly couple in front of them was having difficulty with all their belongings and the woman dropped her bag, spilling most of the contents on the floor, including their cruise cards.

A young man appeared out of nowhere and helped them assemble their things and they were soon on their way with everyone else.

Now seated in the reserved boarding area, Marcus turned to Jenna, saying, "Jenna, how do you know so much about cruising? I would have been totally lost going through this process."

"Marcus, it's not that complicated. My parents have been cruising for years and even took me along when I was in high school. Let me give you a quick fill in before we get on board. First, that black cruise card you have in your hand will be all you need to carry on board. Your wallet and money will go in the safe in our room. When we board and go through ship security, they will scan the card and take your picture, putting you in the ship's computer. From then on the card becomes the key to our cabin, your credit card on board, and your pass to get on and off the ship. You will see other passengers with other colored cards; ours are black indicating we are Elite status. This status is reserved for passengers who have cruised at least 15 cruises and gives you the same perks that passengers in suites have. The agency arranged for this as it will allow us to be most anywhere that Suite passengers are normally accommodated. That way if the Gambioni family leaves their cabin, we will be able to stay in close proximity. There was no way that the entire crew could be told we were CIA, so this was the best way to give us the access we needed without compromising our cover."

Jenna continued and Marcus listened, but kept a watchful eye on the passengers who continued to file in. A commotion at the entrance to the area silenced their conversation and caught their attention. Two security guards were escorting what appeared to be a special contingent. They were ushered through the waiting area and onto the ship.

"Oh, shit!" exclaimed Marcus.

"What's the matter?" asked Jenna.

"Did you recognize that group that just passed by?"

Jenna shook her head no.

"Well, that was the Gambioni contingent. They were all wearing dark glasses but not a very good cover if you know them. The tall man was Franco and the two women were his wife and daughter. Both quite the lookers. The other two guys I assume are bodyguards and one of them is the 'Oh shit.'"

"What do you mean?"

"The short one is Sal Indelicato. He obviously didn't see or recognize me. Just what I worried about and you didn't think was worth being concerned about. Well, there you have it, we could have a problem. He will certainly be surprised about me being married." Then grabbing Jenna's hand, Marcus continued, "By the way, where did the agency get those rings you are wearing? They are pretty flashy."

"Don't get too excited, they are not real. Just paste. But good paste, actually the best costume jewelry one can buy. The Indelicato guy might not be a problem, Marcus. If he knows you, we may be able to get closer to Franco, and he's kind of cute. The Indelicato guy, not Franco."

"What do you mean?"

"Look, he knows you, you're his friend. When we see him on board, you introduce your new wife to him and maybe we get close on the trip."

That might work, thought Marcus.

They were called to board and now another small queue formed up the gangway to ship security. The elderly couple ahead of them appeared to be having problems again locating their cruise cards and they dropped to the back of the line. Looking ahead, Marcus spotted the young man who had helped the elderly couple before.

I wonder how he got that far ahead of the line, thought Marcus. *I can't figure why, but he either looks familiar or reminds me of someone. Oh, well.* His thoughts were quickly interrupted by Jenna, calling, "Marcus, you are holding up the line, keep up."

————•◆•————

They boarded the ship at the Plaza Deck level and proceeded through ship security. Marcus was overwhelmed with the internal décor of the ship as Jenna led him through the deck to the elevators.

"A grand staircase, open plaza area several floors high. Amazing, it's like a five-star hotel inside," he exclaimed. "I would never have believed."

"It gets better," replied Jenna. "We'll go on a tour after we get settled in our cabin."

Getting off the elevator and proceeding down the passage way to their cabin, Marcus noted the mail racks in front of each cabin door. They all had a card denoting the occupants' name and cruise level. "Well, I guess you can't hide who you are or where you live on the ship," he said.

"Well, there is good reason for that. That is how the ship communicates with you and how you can communicate with others. It is the internal mail system. In addition, we will get a daily newspaper delivered each night telling the ship's activities for the coming day," replied Jenna.

As they approached their cabin, Jenna pointed to the card in their mailbox.

Mr. Marcus Peterson
Mrs. Jenna (Adams) Peterson

Seeing that sent a chill through Marcus. Even though it had been ordained, he was not totally sure he was ready for the concept.

Opening the cabin door, Jenna exclaimed joyously, "Great, our bags are already here. We can get settled right away."

Marcus, seeing the Mini Suite sleeping area with twin beds and then the sitting area separated by a TV bar cabinet and a dressing table, commented, "Though it's pretty plush, there isn't much in the way of personal privacy, is there?"

"Look Marcus, if you are concerned, the couch in the sitting area opens up to a bed and that's where I slept when I cruised with my folks. We can even drape a blanket between the TV console and dressing table," replied Jenna with a little annoyance in her voice. Just then the ship's horn sounded.

"Marcus, quick, out on the balcony. We are about to set sail. It's great fun waving at the well-wishers and seeing the well-wishers wave at us. Maybe we can see our favorite family."

"What's a well-wisher?" asked Marcus.

"That's what I call all the people on the dock that wish they were going, but wish us a safe trip," said Jenna as she opened the sliding door to the balcony and they went out. She was so right. Just below them they could see the Gambioni family suite balcony, almost twice the size of theirs, complete with a varnished wood table and chairs plus two chaise lounges. Franco was nowhere in sight but wife and daughter were at the rail enjoying the festivities. Marcus spotted Sal on the balcony next to the Gambionis with binoculars scanning the crowd on the dock and hoped he didn't look up.

"Jenna, back away from the rail. I don't think we want our downstairs neighbors to see us just yet," said Marcus as he stepped back, putting them out of sight from the deck below. "It will be best if we meet them first. Hopefully, we will run into Sal in one of the public areas."

The sounds from the sail-away party on the Sun and Lido decks caused Marcus to look up and to his surprise he spotted that same young man in the crowd at the rail. He was looking down in Sal's direction, not at the people dockside.

I know that guy, but who is he? thought Marcus.

Sipping lattes at the International Café in the atrium on the Plaza Deck, Marcus and Jenna were conversing on all that they had seen on the ship's tour. Jenna reflected on what great fun things there were to do in all the different venues. They were startled by Sal approaching, saying, "Marcus, what are you doing here? How are you? I haven't seen you in years. Well, at least four, I think."

"Sal, sit down. Join us. Let me introduce you to my wife," replied Marcus. "We are on our honeymoon. But you, Sal, I knew you were in the security business, but did we see you with the Gambioni family during boarding? I didn't know you were working for the mob." "Well, that is an interesting story. Franco obviously needs protection. But he doesn't trust his own people so he hires a legitimate security agency and that's me. And the money is great. I could care less where it comes from," responded Sal.

"I would've never thought that. But isn't a cruise a little unusual for a Mafia boss?

"Yes, but it's a present to his wife. They've been married 25 years and she wanted a family vacation. Franco felt it was safer on a ship than going to a resort somewhere and he hired my firm to protect them while on the trip. That's about as much as I know."

Sal obviously doesn't know about the planned meeting in Colombia, thought Marcus, *and I sure can't tell him.*

"How did you and Jenna get together?" asked Sal.

"Oh, we met in college and one thing led to another and here we are married."

"Well, there was a little more to it than that," chimed in Jenna. "We were an item our junior and senior years."

Jenna is really into this role playing, thought Marcus. *I better stay alert for the story that she is dreaming up.*

"Are you married, Sal?" asked Jenna.

"No, the right one just hasn't come along yet. Being in the security business doesn't lend itself to meeting potential lady friends."

"Oh, I don't know about that," said Marcus. "Franco's daughter appears to be quite the dish."

"Hey, Marcus. You're married. You are not supposed to notice those things. And as for me, you never consider getting involved with your clients. Especially in the security business."

"Look, Sal, just because I am on a diet doesn't mean I'm not allowed to read the menu," said Marcus.

"And it sure as hell better stop there," chimed in Jenna.

"You two sure don't sound like newlyweds," said Sal.

"Well, yes, we did just get married but we have been living together for quite a while," said Jenna.

My god! This play-acting is getting quite involved, thought Marcus. *I can't believe the tale she is spinning about us.*

"Look, you two enjoy your latte. I have to get back to relieve my partner," said Sal. And with that, he excused himself and was off.

As Sal left, Marcus looked at Jenna with questioning eyes and said, "Aren't you getting a little carried away with our story?"

"Look, I am just trying to make it sound real. And by the way, I think your friend is a nice guy. I hope when this is all over, I can see him again as me," said Jenna. Looking at her watch, she continued, "Bottoms up, we have one more chore to do. We have to go see the maître d' about a table assignment."

"Table assignment? What's that all about? Don't we just go to the Windows Court on the Lido Deck you showed me?"

"We will probably use it sometimes maybe for breakfast or lunch but we still will want a place in one of the dining rooms, preferably where and when the Gambionis are. That opens two options we have to scope out. Option one is what is called traditional dining. That is in the Portofino Dining Room I showed you on the Fiesta Deck aft and it is served either at 6:00 or 8:15. If you choose that option, you are assigned a specific table and are expected to go only there. Option two is what is called Flexible Dining. That is served in the Crown Dining Room on the Plaza deck from 5:30 to 10:00. It's like restaurant dining in that you go anytime or make a reservation anytime depending on availability. You have the option to make a standing reservation if you like. Now we have to find out just what the Gambioni family is intending to do and see if we can tag along."

"How are we going to do that?" responded Marcus.

"Hopefully, we can find out from the maître d' and make a similar set of arrangements. Come on, let's go."

With that, they were off to the Contessa Grill where the maître d' was holding court.

"Jenna, is this the norm?" asked Marcus. He was overwhelmed with the opulence of the Portofino Dining Room, the service, the menu, the food. "Is every meal like this?" he continued as he washed the last bite of the Grand Marnier soufflé down with his cappuccino.

"Oh, yes," said Jenna, "and best watch your quantities. You don't have to have every course, you know. If you are not careful, you will shortly grow out of the new wardrobe the agency just bought you."

Jenna had been right in her call. The Gambioni family went for fixed dining due to its privacy and she cleverly had the maitre d' assign them a table for two in close proximity to the Gambioni table. All through the meal, Marcus could hardly take his eyes off Franco's daughter and Jenna caught him staring again.

"Marcus! Be careful," said Jenna. "We are supposed to keep an eye on the Gambionis, not stare them down." She paused. "Oh, the Gambioni's are leaving. It looks like Sal is bringing the daughter over to meet us."

"Angelina, I would like you to meet the Petersons, a newly-wed couple on their honeymoon," said Sal as he approached the Petersons' table. "Marcus and I grew up together in the same neighborhood."

Marcus and Jenna immediately stood up and after exchanging pleasantries, both couples exited the dining room together.

———•◦•———

It had been a long day, and Jenna and Marcus settled into their digs on board. They reconfigured the Mini Suite, hanging a curtain between the bed area and the living area. Opening the couch to a bed afforded them two semi-private sleeping areas. Jenna had crashed while Marcus sat out on the balcony contemplating all that had happened and what the future could be.

Angelina, what a fitting name. She could be an 'Angelina Jolie,' thought Marcus. *It was difficult taking my eyes off her when Sal introduced us. I have never felt instantly attracted to someone before. Jenna was right in openly kidding me about it as it made things a little easier.*

If Sal or the Gambioni family ever knew we were CIA, we would be in real trouble. This assignment could get complicated. It's a far cry from 'Mission Impossible' but it sure beats sitting at a desk in Manhattan.

Suddenly Marcus sat up straight in the deck lounge chair. A new thought jumped in his head and he mumbled out loud, "Oh, my God, I know that face."

———•◦•———

Marcus slipped past the sleeping Jenna and went to the fitness center. When he finished his routine, he called their stateroom to wake her up and told her to meet him at the Windows Court for breakfast. They went through the buffet line and settled at a table by the Calypso Pool.

"The fitness center is great. I'll be able to stay in pretty good shape. Maybe burn off the calories from all that food. How did you sleep? You were certainly sawing wood when I left this morning," said Marcus.

"I slept great but I did hear you go out on the balcony before I fell asleep," said Jenna. "What was that all about?"

"That's what I want to talk to you about. I was sitting out there going over everything that had happened in my mind when all of a sudden it came to me. That guy! The one we thought slipped on the ship, and later I saw on the upper deck during the sail-away party. Well, I finally placed his face. He's associated with a Colombian drug cartel."

Jenna's eyes opened wide and her jaw dropped.

"Remember the briefing we got before leaving? It showed how the drug smuggling organizations reincarnated themselves into over 300 smaller organizations being operated by the lieutenants of the disbanded Medellín and Cali cartels. They showed us pictures of some of the arrests in the crackdown on those major cartels. Well, he was in one of the pictures," continued Marcus.

"Oh, no. What's he doing on the ship?" asked Jenna.

"I don't know but when we were sailing away, he appeared to be more interested in the Gambioni balcony than the people on shore. Remember our primary assignment is to determine who Franco contacts in Colombia. Get pictures, names, whatever and report back. It is all part of the agency effort to identify which of those 300-plus smaller traffickers are dealing in the US. I know we weren't supposed to contact the agency until our return to maintain our cover, but we may have to break that order."

Jenna was about to respond when a young staff member came up to their table, saying,

"I believe you're the Petersons, Jenna and Marcus?"

"Yes, but how did you recognize us?" said Marcus.

"You recall your picture was taken when you boarded the ship? We know what everyone looks like," she responded.

"I'm sorry. What can we do for you?" said Marcus.

"I am Myla, special assistant to the captain. He would like to meet with you both as soon as possible."

"What's this all about? Have we done something wrong?" said Marcus.

"No, not at all, but it's best you speak to him directly. If you are finished with your breakfast, I will show you to the bridge."

CHAPTER 2

At Sea

Both Jenna and Marcus were overwhelmed with the size and spaciousness of the bridge. "The bridge has sure changed since I used to cruise with my parents," said Jenna as Myla led them through the entry, passing the communication and alarm center and chart table. The bridge proper was quite expansive, for it extended past the decks on both starboard and port sides, allowing for a full view aft.

"It's huge!" commented Marcus.

Captain Hempsell and another officer were seated together at one end of the bridge away from the control positions and as Myla brought Jenna and Marcus in to them, the captain rose and extended his hand, saying, "Welcome aboard, agents Adams and Peterson. This is my security officer, Howard Smith. Please sit down."

"Thank you, Captain, and call me Marcus, please sir. Is there something wrong?" said Marcus.

As they sat down, Myla excused herself, and the captain, ignoring Marcus's question, said, "When your agency made arrangements for your sailing, I was briefed on your mission and its covert nature. You should be aware that other than myself, only my security officer and Myla have been briefed. That being said, you should also be aware that therefore the crew at large will be extending the standard considerations given all our passengers. And no more. If you need any additional support of any kind, your contact should be Myla."

"Understood, and thank you, sir," responded Marcus and Jenna almost in unison.

"Now I wanted to speak to both of you about an incident that occurred during embarkation, and its impact was not comprehended before sailing. It was brought to my attention shortly thereafter and quite possibly, one of you or your agency may be able to provide some assistance. I'll let my security officer explain."

"It appears we have a stowaway aboard and we have not been able to locate him," said Howard Smith.

"I don't understand," said Marcus.

"Let me explain," continued Howard. "You remember our boarding process. There is the time when you check in and then actually board the ship. If you remember, you presented all of your identification and boarding passes at registration, where you were issued a cruise card. You then boarded the ship and your picture was taken as you passed through ship's security. That picture was stored with your cruise card in our computer. Well, it is now clear that someone followed the actual boarding process with someone else's cruise card yesterday. Just before sailing we boarded an elderly couple that had lost their cruise cards somewhere on the way to the boarding ramp and had to be issued new ones. When they went through ship's security, their cruise cards brought up a different picture from them and would not allow their picture to be taken. All this was rectified, but we realized an imposter had boarded the ship. Now we have over 2500 passengers and 1200 crew, so finding this imposter may not be an easy job even though we have his picture."

While the Security officer was relating the story, Marcus's facial expression changed from attentive curiosity to certainty as he realized he had witnessed much of what was described. He immediately responded, "We know who he is. We believe he is a Colombian and a member of one of their drug cartels."

"I believe your mission and our stowaway issue may have just become entwined."

After their meeting on the bridge the captain arranged for a secure phone connection with the agency in New York. Following detailed discussions, Jenna and Marcus found their assignment had become considerably more complicated.

The agency was definitely interested in the stowaway as based on Marcus's description. They could only narrow it down to him originally being part of the Cali cartel. Why he was on the ship and whether that had anything to do with a Gambioni cartel meeting was to be determined. Currently, the agency was not aware of any internal wars or rivalries existing between the smaller cartels trafficking drugs with the US but cautioned Marcus to be alert and careful as such rivalries could erupt at any time and be quite fierce.

Huddled in the mini office that was provided them, digesting their agency call and planning their approach, Marcus said, "It sounds like our home office is still in the process of trying to sort things out concerning the new cartel operations now existing in Colombia and our little mission is to feed data to a much larger activity in process."

"Yes, and I don't think they expected our mission to involve more than one cartel," said Jenna. "Our stowaway could either be an advance contact for the Gambioni meeting or could be from a rival cartel."

"One thing's for sure, we will definitely have to be on our toes in St. Thomas and Aruba as a meeting could occur well before we get to Colombia. In fact, a meeting in Cartagena may not occur at all," said Marcus.

"If this guy is from a rival cartel, could the Gambionis be in danger?" asked Jenna. "Should we be letting Sal in on what's going on?"

"Whoa, Jenna. Our cover is paramount, and if we did, it would surely complicate Sal's relationship with the Gambionis. I am sure Franco would not appreciate someone working for him who had a close friend in the CIA. Remember our mission: watchful bystanders."

———

Marcus had established a basic morning routine. A mile on a treadmill, three sets of twelve reps on eight machines followed by time in the sauna, steam room and then relaxation on a heated stone bed in the Body Oasis Spa. He would then meet Jenna at the Windows Court for breakfast. This morning proved a little different. His alarm watch went off and as he rose from the heated stone bed, a vision of loveliness emerged from the steam room. Angelina, dressed in a sparse bikini and shimmering with perspiration, said, "Good morning, Marcus. What a surprise so early in the morning. Is Jenna here?"

Marcus was relieved he had a loose towel thrown over himself as he was instantly aroused. Angelina was truly a vision of loveliness and could well have been a model for Vogue. "Why no, Angelina, I will be meeting her at the Windows Court for breakfast. She is not really an early riser. Do you do this every morning?"

"I usually start my day with stretching exercises in either my cabin or in the fitness center and follow that with the steam room and a cold shower. It's my wakeup call to my body." Then with a mischievous smile, Angelina continued, "Does it look woken up to you?"

Would I love to wake that body up, thought Marcus. Then, ignoring her last comment, he said, "I'll tell Jenna we met and about your routine, but I'm sure she would want no part of it."

With that, Angelina went into one of the showers and Marcus

quickly exited to the men's locker room thinking, *What a bummer having to pretend I'm married to Jenna.*

The passageway back to the locker room was dimly lit as the full lighting didn't go on until the spa staff arrived at seven o'clock. Marcus was almost knocked down making his way to the locker room as an attendant rushed past him shouting, "*Perdone, señor.*"

The door to the locker room was partially open. Marcus pushed on it and found it difficult to open; something was blocking it. With a little force he squeezed in and to his surprise found another attendant slumped on the floor, holding his throat and gasping for air.

Kneeling down, Marcus tried to calm him, saying, "Breathe slowly, easy." When the attendant's breathing became normal, Marcus continued, "You are a lucky man. You suffered a martial arts blow to the throat used to incapacitate someone. Your assailant could have crushed your trachea, which can cause death from asphyxiation. What happened?"

"I don't know. It was all so fast. I was stacking towels and this guy comes in, grabs my crew badge and before I could say something, I was on the floor gasping for air."

"Yes, he hit you with a very fast chop to the throat. Here, let me help you up."

"Thanks, I think I am OK except for a sore neck."

"Good, I would report it to your supervisor. Are you sure you can make it back?"

"Yes, and thanks again." With that said, the attendant was gone.

Marcus raced to the reception area phone to call Security Officer Smith's ship cell number.

"Howard, we have a new issue. Our Colombian stowaway has a crew badge and, by the way, he may be a ninja warrior."

Dead silence on the other end was followed by a loud, "What?"

"Seriously," replied Marcus, "he appears to be martial-arts

trained." Marcus continued to report what he had just experienced and Howard replied, "It will take time to locate him. With a crew badge he will be able to move rapidly through the crew access passageways unnoticed, especially during the day since traffic for required services is pretty heavy. But I assure you, we will find him."

"Well, caution your people to take care. As of now, we know he can be dangerous. When you catch him, I would like to be able to question him."

Finishing the call, Marcus made his way to the Windows Court for breakfast. As he approached Jenna with his breakfast tray in hand, he was greeted with, "What happened to you? Get carried away on the treadmill watching TV or fall asleep in the spa?"

Marcus responded, "Jenna, you just wouldn't believe!"

The Gambioni suite was one of the Grand Suites on board. Very luxurious, separate sitting area, coffee table, sofa bed, wet bar, and desk with personal computer. The sitting area doubled as Angelina's bedroom and was reconfigured back to a sitting room by their room steward while she was at the spa in the early morning. She would call his pager when she left. The heavy curtain pulled at night separating the bedroom area allowed for the transition to be accomplished with minimal disturbance to Franco and his wife.

An exclusive breakfast was provided in Raffaello's restaurant every morning for suite passengers that included mimosas, which his wife and Angelina loved. Franco, however, preferred having his *colazione* in their cabin. This morning was no different. A wonderful spread was delivered precisely at 9:00: a frittata baked with parmesan and eggs (the garlic of which permeated the room when it arrived), a basket of *fette biscottate* and *cornetti* (croissants) with a side of apricot marmalade. Best of all, a pot of strong Italian coffee accompanied by a pot of warm milk. Angelina had returned from breakfast and was enjoying a second cup of coffee with her father and one of his croissants with jam, when Franco decided to log on to the internet. Angelina settled on the sofa reading the shipboard daily patter to see what was available to do when she was startled by her father's scream.

"*Merda! Affanculo!* Angelina, where is your mother?" yelled Franco.

"Father, what is the problem? Mother is up at the hairdresser. Swearing won't help but maybe I can," said Angelina.

"I'm pissed. I can't get this damn computer to log on to the internet. We are supposed to have shipboard access. I need to contact Luigi. It's important business."

"What is our business?" asked Angelina.

"You don't need to know that. I have told you a thousand times. Just get me on the internet."

Like many Mafiosi, Franco had tried to shield Angelina from Mafia activities. It was never discussed in her presence. She had always attended private schools and went to college in Massachusetts. If she was aware, he did not know.

Franco was not at all proficient in using a PC. As a Don of one of the largest and strongest crime families in New York, he did business in the normal Cosa Nostra fashion: face to face or through his *consigliere*. Verbal communication left no paper trail, which was the rule of thumb. That was the real reason for the trip, though mother and daughter had no idea. Luigi, his underboss, had assured him that all would be well locally but they could communicate by email if necessary, but then with guarded wording.

"Father, you have to sign in to your shipboard internet account first, then the internet, then your email. Here, let me show you."

But before Angelina could sit down in front of the computer, the cabin door opened and in came Franco's wife. "Adriana, thank

God you are here. Angelina, go somewhere. Enjoy the ship, your mother will help me," said Franco.

"Go, Angelina. I will tend to your father," said Adriana, as Angelina went out the cabin door.

Adriana turned and said in a very annoyed voice, "Franco, you promised! This was to be a real vacation, no business. What are you on the computer for?"

"Calm down, Adriana. I just have to touch base with Luigi. I want to know how that new capo is working out. He is supposed to be running the numbers in Queens. That's important income."

As he spoke, his mind was racing with other thoughts. *What I really need from Luigi is if he has heard of any change in the contact information for my meeting. This was to be provided verbally on board by a messenger but we are two days out and I have been approached by no one. If and when Adriana finds out I am having a business meeting on this trip, she will really be upset. Maybe I can buy her some emerald jewelry in Cartagena. Hopefully, that will placate her.*

"Adriana, help me here, please," he said.

———•◦•———

Marcus was amazed at how quickly he had become accustomed to living with Jenna. She was so right; it was no different from being home with his sister.

"Marcus, help me here, please," said Jenna as she came out of the dressing area in front of the bathroom. "I can't reach the zipper in the back of this dress. Hey, your tux looks pretty cool. I'm glad we got you a tie and cummerbund to complement my dress. It should make us look like typical newlyweds."

"Maybe so," said Marcus. "Turn around, and explain again about this 'Welcome Aboard Party' we are going to. Will the Gambionis be there?"

"Yes, and when I spoke to Myla, she told me they would be

getting a special invitation and would be admitted prior to everyone else."

"How and why, what's that all about?"

"Typically on all cruises and certainly this one. The second night out is formal night and the captain hosts a 'Welcome Aboard Party' for everyone. You get to meet the captain and he usually introduces his crew and everyone is treated to free cocktails. There will be a queue to get in. Everyone gets an invitation; ours is over on the dressing table. You bring it along, hand it to the crew member at the entrance and he hands it to Myla, who introduces you to the captain and sometimes they take your picture. Which, of course, they will be happy to sell you later. The special invitation allows the Gambionis to avoid standing in line. Put the invite in your pocket, Marcus, and let's be out of here. We don't want to be at the end of the queue."

———————

The Cabaret Lounge was jammed with passengers, mostly in formal attire. The melodious sound of the Duchess orchestra, playing Duke Ellington's "Satin Doll," provided an undertone to the raucous conversation permeating the room. Dispersed heavily through the crowd was a serving staff with trays of cocktail choices and hors d'oeuvres. This staff appeared huge, probably recruited from all the other lounges on board. Audible conversation was only possible on a close one-on-one basis.

The Gambioni contingent had settled themselves at two cocktail tables in the back of the room by the bar farthest from the stage and quite close to the entrance. This could provide for an unnoticed early exit when the welcoming group relocated to the stage for the festivities. Jenna and Marcus selected a table in the same area but somewhat distant from the Gambionis. Sal had noticed them when they arrived and smiled, giving an indication of recognition. The music stopped and as the captain and Myla walked up to the stage, most passenger conversation quieted.

Leaning over to Marcus, Jenna said, "Myla whispered in my ear when we were in the reception line that they haven't found the stowaway yet. And if he had done anything to his appearance, he could well be with the waiting staff. Worse, because of crew changes, even most of the waiting staff aren't aware of each other on the first day out. She asked that we keep a lookout as we are really the only ones who have seen him first hand."

As Jenna was talking, Marcus was watching the Gambionis being served their drinks by a waiter with a shaved head. Then everything appeared to happen at once. Captain Hempsell started his welcoming speech, causing all attention to be drawn to the stage. The waiter serving the drinks to the Gambionis laid a receipt on their table and left. Looking at it, Franco motioned to Sal and they both got up and left the lounge.

"You stay and keep an eye on the Gambioni women. I'm going to follow Sal and Franco. I can't be sure but their waiter could have been the stowaway with his head shaved," said Marcus as he jumped up and left.

When he got out in the hall, there was no sign of Franco or Sal. They literally had vanished. There were three directions they could have gone plus the elevators, but looking around, he saw no one. Racing back into the Cabaret Lounge, he saw that Jenna had joined Adriana and Angelina. The crew introductions had been completed and the officers were leaving the stage. Marcus spotted Security Officer Smith coming toward him.

"Howard, I think I saw our stowaway. He shaved his head and appears to be posing as a waiter," said Marcus as they approached each other. Looking around, he continued, "but I don't see him now."

Security Officer Smith immediately went through the crew access door behind the bar, leaving Marcus a little stunned. As he turned to Jenna, Adriana, and Angelina, he was surprised to see Franco and Sal coming back to the table as if nothing had occurred. As he approached their table, Sal observed the questioning expression on Marcus's face and said, "Nature called."

That was the one place I didn't think to look, thought Marcus. *The men's restroom was located right outside the Cabaret Lounge entrance. How dumb could I be?*

At that moment a sound of chimes came over the PA system, followed by the announcement, "Dinner is being served in the Portofino Dining Room."

The Gambionis and Sal immediately got up and, passing Jenna and Marcus, Franco smiled, saying, "Ciao."

Marcus was delighted that Adriana asked if she and Angelina could join them in going to the show in the Duchess Theatre. It was supposed to feature the entire cruise cast of singers and dancers in their version of the "British Invasion."

Wow! thought Marcus, *a chance to be with Angelina.*

Sensing Marcus's thoughts, Jenna squeezed his hand as they walked toward the theatre and whispered, "Easy there, remember we are supposed to be married."

Following the show Adriana excused herself to join Franco in their cabin while Angelina chose to go with Jenna and Marcus to the Voyagers Lounge for a nightcap.

Later, when Sal caught up with them, he was surprised to see Marcus and Angelina on the dance floor and Jenna alone sipping her drink. "Hey, Jenna. What's going on? Hubby desert you?" said Sal.

"Supposedly not," responded Jenna in a somewhat annoyed tone. "Angelina wanted to dance and Marcus thought it impolite not to accommodate her."

"Well, hey, I'm available, the music is great. Let's do it."

It was quite late when the band finished their final set and the two couples retired. Jenna grabbed her pj's, saying, "Me first," as soon as they got to their cabin, so Marcus found himself out on the balcony contemplating the day as he waited for his turn at the bathroom.

He was surprised to see what appeared to be a sizable yacht paralleling the ship's travel not too far away. But then realizing they were due in St. Thomas in the morning, he figured it was just part of the normal sailing traffic in and out of that island.

I'll mention it to Howard when I see him in the morning, thought Marcus. *It did appear closer than you would expect any boat to get to an ocean liner speeding along at 17 knots.* He and Jenna had planned on meeting Howard for breakfast to discuss the St. Thomas port call and how they were going to track the Gambionis.

"It's all yours," came the call from Jenna.

CHAPTER 3

St. Thomas

It was a typical glorious day in the Caribbean, not a cloud in the sky and a soft cool breeze that helped mitigate the humidity. The Golden Duchess slowly moved toward the WICO terminal pier where preparations for its arrival were already underway. Marcus didn't dally this morning when he finished his exercise routine: it was a quick shower and on to breakfast. However, the thought did cross his mind that it would have been nice to have another chance meeting with Angelina, maybe in the sauna. Security Officer Smith had already joined Jenna for breakfast at the Windows Court and when Marcus approached, called out, "Good morning, Marcus. Come, we have much to plan for." As Marcus sat down, he continued, "It appears our stowaway is no more. We believe he jumped ship, probably when we slowed down approaching St. Thomas. The crew found some clothes on the aft crew deck this morning."

"Well, if he did, that yacht I saw last night could have picked him up," replied Marcus, and he continued to describe the yacht and how surprised he was as it appeared to be tracking quite close to the Golden Duchess.

Security Officer Smith listened intently, making a mental note to check with the bridge to see if anything about the close encounter was recorded in the ship's log. Then he responded, "Well, our stowaway was not only a good swimmer but very capable of finding places to hide. When you gave me the description at the reception last night, we initiated an immediate all-crew vigil but to no avail. Of course, there are a multitude of places he could hide for a short time."

During this short dialog, Jenna listened but appeared anxious and interrupted the conversation with, "Look, we will dock in an hour, and from what we learned from Sal and Angelina last night, keeping track of the Gambionis will be a challenge today."

"Yes, Angelina and Adriana are signed up for the sightseeing and Blackbeard's Castle excursion while Sal said he and Franco were going to some marina to look at a yacht that he had heard about that was up for sale," said Marcus.

"That would probably be at the Yacht Haven Grande Marina," said Howard. "That's the only marina that handles large yachts in St. Thomas and it's right next to the WICO terminal where we will dock. We can walk there."

"I called Myla last night and had her sign me up for the same shore excursion," said Jenna, "so I should be able to cover Angelina and Adriana." "I think we have a plan," said Howard. "Marcus, I will meet you at the disembarkation deck as soon as its location is announced; I believe it will be on deck 4. It will be a while before the excursions get organized as they normally meet in the Voyagers Lounge and proceed to disembarkation and the buses by tour group number. We can be on shore well before the passengers in general and position ourselves in one of the cafes that overlook the marina. That should allow us to monitor Sal and Franco's travels. This yacht-buying story could be a cover for a meeting."

The Golden Duchess was finally secure at the cruise ship terminal. Its size and structure allowed all passengers on the port side a spectacular overlook of St. Thomas's Charlotte Amalie

Harbor. The ship's berthing position placed it immediately adjacent to the Yacht Haven Grande Marina, a favorite Caribbean port for the rich and famous. The number and size of the yachts moored there was always an amazement to first-time visitors.

Franco and Sal had been given instructions to proceed to the Reina del Mar that would be moored at slip A10 in the marina, the yacht supposedly owned by Pablo Londoño, the drug lord who wanted to meet with Franco. "There it is, Mr. Ganbioni," said Sal as he pointed it out to Franco from the Gambioni cabin balcony. "It's that large one at the end of the pier. I checked the slip location on the shore excursion handout provided with the ship newsletter last night."

"I see it, and I think I best have some insurance," said Franco as he dialed his cell phone.

"Luigi, have Romano fly to Aruba day after tomorrow. Ship gets into port at 8:00. I want him dockside!!!!"

"Mr. Gambioni, you don't have to yell. I am sure Mr. Santori can hear you. Sound travels out here on the balcony," said Sal.

"Right," said Franco to Sal, then back on the cell, "Luigi, I have a preliminary meeting today on the Londoño yacht. In fact, I can see the damn boat from here. Pablo will not be there but could be in Aruba. The messenger was vague with details other than this get together was to simply discuss timing and location of a meeting with Pablo in Colombia. I am beginning to believe we should handle this potential relationship as we normally do at home. That is where we normally have preliminary meetings between Romano and their *consigliere*, if Pablo has one. I am going to suggest this occur in Aruba and I'll call you later, before we sail, to confirm."

Ending the call and looking at Sal, Franco said, "Is your partner going with the girls on the tour? I don't want them left alone while on shore. Even though they will be part of an organized ship's shore excursion, I have no feel for the Londoño cartel's business practices. I have heard hostages have been involved in some Colombian drug cartel negotiations."

"Really? Well, yes, that's taken care of. My partner is signed up for the excursion and will be with them the whole time they are off the ship. By the way, Mr. Gambioni, won't your wife be upset if she finds out we are going to a business meeting?"

"Look, Indelicato, your job is to keep me and my family alive, not meddle in my personal affairs. We are going to look at a yacht I might want to buy and that's the story. Their excursion ends up at the Hotel 1829 and we will meet them at the bar there as we planned. Now let's get off this damn ship and go to our meeting."

"Yes, sir," responded Sal and they were off.

———•·•———

Marcus and Security Officer Howard Smith were off the ship with the crew.

"We are well ahead of the passengers," said Howard. "It will be at least another half hour before disembarkation of passengers starts. The crew will be setting up a photo area with some props to offer pictures of each passenger as they leave the ship."

"Jenna will love that. She is really into this cruising bit. She did a lot of trips with her folks when she was young," responded Marcus.

The walk to the Yacht Haven Grande area was quick and Marcus and Howard located themselves at a table at the "Fat Turtle" overlooking the Marina, the only restaurant open in the morning. It had a fairly good view of anyone entering the Yacht Haven Grande area and it also afforded a good view of most of the yachts docked in the marina.

Marcus was sipping his second cappuccino when he spotted them. Sal and Franco entered the area and proceeded immediately out to the yachts.

"It looks like they're heading to the yacht moored at very end of the pier. Oh, my God, that's the yacht I saw last night tracking with us. I didn't notice it when we looked down on the marina from onboard the ship this morning, but seeing it now, there is no question. That's it," said Marcus.

"Well, it looks like that's where they're going," said Howard.

Marcus, pulling a small set of binoculars out of his jacket pocket and focusing on Franco and Sal, continued, "Someone's helping them on board and they appear to be going right into the cabin."

"Well, I guess if you were going to buy a yacht you would want to look around some." said Howard, still believing that Franco and Sal were doing just what Sal had said they were going to do.

Watching the activity through the binoculars, Marcus reported, "They have powered up and two crew members are out on deck releasing the forward and aft lines."

"Come on, Marcus, they are probably just going for a spin around the harbor. I would certainly want a test ride if I were thinking about buying it. I think our action is over. They appear to be doing just as reported and there is certainly no indication of any clandestine activity.

I have to get back to the ship and I suggest you try to team back up with Jenna and the Gambioni women."

Marcus, still watching the yacht through the binoculars as it pulled away from the dock and proceeded out of the marina into the harbor at large said, "Ah, I can see its name: Reina del Mar, Queen of the Sea. That sounds familiar for some reason. Oh, wait, we have an issue. Our stowaway appears to be on board; he just showed up on deck with Sal Indelicato."

—————•+•—————

As they boarded the tour bus, ship side, Adriana was delighted to be welcomed by the tour guide in perfect Italian and directed to the front tour guide seat. Jenna and Angelina boarded and took a seat together further in the back. The tour guide explained to Adriana that she was part of the ship's staff and from Sicily.

"My husband's family was originally from Sicily," said Adriana. "That was several generations back. I don't believe we have any contact any more with relatives we might have there now."

"I can't believe that," said the tour guide. "There is always a family contact somewhere. I am sure if you pressed your husband, you would find that one exists. The family ties with those that immigrated to America from Sicily are never broken."

"What was that all about?" asked Jenna as she and Angelina sat down.

"Oh, that's my little fun. I signed up for all the shore excursions on our first day at sea and met her. She is part of the ship's shore excursion staff and when I found out she was from Sicily I thought it would be fun to surprise my mother. She thought it was a great idea and agreed to take the tour. The staff pretty much trades around leading the different shore excursions so it was no problem. Where's Marcus? I thought he would be with you."

"He wasn't feeling that great this morning, and the thought of driving around winding roads in a tour bus just didn't sound appealing. Hopefully, he will join us at Blackbeard's castle where the land tour ends or at the Hotel 1829. It is at the base of the castle. Do you speak Italian?"

"Not really, oh, very little. We don't speak it at home. My mother does and when my grandmother visits, they chat away in Italian when they want to talk about something they don't want me to know about. By the way, what do you and Marcus do? You mentioned that you met each other at work but never said what work?"

Now I hope I don't screw this up. We rehearsed the answer we would give if ever asked, but if she asks details, I could be in trouble, thought Jenna.

"We both work for a real estate management firm that manages luxury apartments on the East side. Marcus is in sales and I work in finance. Not very exciting jobs but it's a living," responded Jenna, hoping no further questions would be asked. Her fear was quickly mitigated as the tour guide started her spiel and the bus took off on the tour.

————•◦•————

Franco Gambioni had little if any knowledge of Colombian culture or the fact that drug cartels cut across all levels of Colombian society. He did not expect to witness their cultural mores in dealing with a drug cartel. Family plays a major role in business associations, which is similar to the Italian Mafia. However, contrary to the Italian Mafia, where women are generally shielded from operations, Colombian women are strong, politically active and may play major roles. As such, he and Sal were completely taken aback as they entered the sumptuously appointed interior of the Londoño yacht.

"Welcome aboard the Reina del Mar, Señor Gambioni. I am Señora Londoño and I believe you already have met my half brother, personal body guard and messenger, Ricardo," said a very comely smiling Hispanic woman standing next to the stowaway and extending her hand. "Please sit down."

Franco was beside himself shaking her hand and sitting down, saying, "Thank you" and thinking, *What have I gotten into? Well, at least she speaks English.*

She proceeded with the standard Colombian greeting dialog, asking about how Franco was feeling, was his wife enjoying the trip, and asking about their daughter.

Franco politely responded to the small talk but was very uncomfortable, wondering where all this was leading. He was not at all expecting to be greeted by a very attractive woman displaying an air of authority and complete control.

Suddenly the smile disappeared and her expression became seriously stern and looking at Franco but addressing Ricardo, she said, "Ricardo, take Señor Indelicato on a tour of the yacht. Señor Gambioni and I wish to talk."

This was spoken as an order. Then addressing Franco in a

much less severe tone, she said, "Señor, I understand you wish to do business with us and would like to meet with my husband. Let us discuss how this may be possible and arranged."

As Franco listened, his mind began to wander. *Is this for real? Does she call the shots? Do I have to initially negotiate with her? I am not at all comfortable with this situation.*

Señora Londoño continued, "You understand, due to security reasons both internal and external, Pablo never leaves the confines of our country. Dealing with the law enforcement activities and competing cartels requires constant vigilance. As such, I handle all external communication for Pablo. The Reina del Mar is our floating headquarters out of the country. Its crew is armed and well trained and it is equipped with only the most up-to-date communication equipment."

Then, reading the very concerned expression on Franco's face, she continued,

"Señor Gambioni, if you are uncomfortable with this, I am sure we will have no problem finding other organizations to handle our product in the US."

This woman is something else, thought Franco. Then displaying his warmest Italian smile, he said, "Senora, please. Let us discuss my future meeting with Pablo."

The Reina del Mar had no sooner docked than Franco was off and on his cell phone, walking with Sal towards town. "Luigi, you must have Romano book a flight to Aruba as soon as possible. We have an unexpected issue here. I just met with Senora Londoño, Pablo's very attractive wife and obviously number two in command. Evidently this is not unusual in the South American cartels. Although initially quite pleasant, she can be as hard as nails and definitely one tough lady. I explained to her that the Mafia mode of operation is that we have a *consigliere* who is my legal advisor and has detailed knowledge of our syndicate's operations meet with a similar representative of any organization we are planning on doing business with. I further explained that it is customary such that final meetings between bosses could be focused only on the issues that had to be negotiated and resolved. She agreed with the concept and Romano should meet with her tomorrow on the Reina del Mar. The yacht will be docked at the Renaissance Marina. They will be expecting him. They now understand how Mafia business is conducted and will try our way."

There was silence on the other end. "Luigi, are you there?"

"Yes, Franco, I'm making notes and listening."

Franco continued, "They obviously will try to do future business with other syndicates. Look, the Golden Duchess docks in Aruba day after tomorrow. We will talk again over the phone at that time. Now let me be clear. At this point, Adriana must not know we spoke or that Romano came down. I want the meeting in Cartagena to be an accidental coincidence and called by Londoño. Make it happen."

Franco still used an old flip cell phone despite continued badgering by his daughter to get a smart one. Flipping it closed and looking at Sal, he said, "Remember, Sal, our story. What we saw today appeared to be an interesting yacht but I want to do a little more research and if it shows up in Aruba I may take another look at it."

"Yes, sir, Mr. Gambioni. The Hotel 1829 is just down this block. We should be there shortly."

———— • • ————

Marcus got to the Hotel 1829 well before anyone else. This allowed him to rap with the bartender and learn a little about the hotel, its history, and its clientele. Turns out that it is one of the local watering holes. Tourists are well on their way to their ships before the locals arrive for happy hour. Being of Scandinavian ancestry, Marcus was fascinated to find out that the Virgin

Islands had belonged to Denmark and the US didn't purchase them until 1917. The hotel was originally built for the bride of a French sea captain and wasn't completed till 1829, hence the name. Converted to a hotel, it has only 15 rooms, which range from large suites to cozy hideaways with balconies. The bar was formerly the kitchen of the old mansion and its intimate ambiance generates thoughts of a Gable, Hemingway or Errol Flynn sitting at the bar hitting on a sweet young tourist. This environment had Marcus's subconscious running wild. *What a terrific hideaway to run off to with the likes of Angelina,* he thought.

His daydream seemed to take life as he felt soft hands cover his eyes and Angelina calling out, "Surprise, we are here."

Startled, he turned to find Jenna's hands on his face and the Gambioni women standing in the doorway, all laughing. "You thought I was Angelina, didn't you?" whispered Jenna into Marcus's ear. Her thoughts were, *Marcus, you won't think of anyone but me by the end of this cruise.*

The scene was now interrupted by the arrival of Sal and Franco. Franco announced to all, "Please, be seated. The drinks are on me. I visited a wonderful yacht today. Adriana, I know you are not keen on having a boat but this was just fabulous. I am so sure you would love it."

"You didn't buy it, did you?" responded Adriana.

"No, No. I have to do more research on it but I just wanted to tell you about it. How was the tour?"

Marcus rolled his eyes and looked at Sal to see if there was any reaction, thinking,

The Gambioni wife and daughter appear to be unaware of Franco's real actions. I wonder just how involved Sal is. Just providing security or really part of the mob?

———•·•———

It was hot and humid in St. Thomas and relief came only from the gentle ocean breeze if you were close to the water's edge. The

Golden Duchess did not leave port until well after eight, though the scheduled departure had been five. Crew changes no longer were accomplished in the continental US because of lengthy custom processing and, as such, St. Thomas was the first port where the Golden Duchess could accomplish this in a reasonable period of time. The deferred departure was due to waiting for a delayed flight carrying critical crew members joining the ship.

Jenna and Marcus sat out on their balcony enjoying the breeze generated by sailing and recapped their activities during the day.

"I am not sure you were made aware but in my briefing before we left, I was informed that as Charlotte Amalie was the capital of the Virgin Islands, we had a central office for Caribbean operations here. After following the travels of Sal and Franco this morning, when Howard went back to the ship I went into the office. Our initial assignment is practically over."

"What do you mean? How can it be?" responded Jenna.

"Well, like I told you before, we saw Franco and Sal get on the yacht Reina del Mar, the boat he has Adriana thinking he wants to buy. The staff at the office did a little research and, voilà, it's registered to Pablo Londoño, one of the Colombian drug cartel bosses. Basically, our assignment was to find out who Franco was going to meet with, so we are done."

"Really, do we get to finish the cruise? Do we have to get off at the next port?"

Hearing the concerned tone of Jenna's voice and seeing the questioning look on her face, Marcus smiled. He had no idea that Jenna had another agenda on this cruise that was far from accomplished. "Yes and no, to answer your questions," responded Marcus, and then in a serious tone continued, "Our assignment has just become more complex. They want pictures, recorded conversations, and names of other cartel members, anything and everything associated with Franco's interfaces with the Colombian cartel."

"Awesome," responded Jenna with an expression of excitement.

"I was able to pick up some additional equipment which I will go over with you tomorrow while we are at sea. The agency feels that, due to the relationship we have established with the Gambioni family on board, we are in a unique position to gain this information."

Totally surprising Marcus, Jenna leaped out of her deck chair, pulled Marcus out of his and put her arms around him and with a voice of pure delight said into his ear, "Marcus, we are becoming real agents. We could be like the Harts of that old TV series Hart to Hart." Then, sensing Marcus's hesitant reaction, she dropped her hands, saying, "I'm sorry. I get a little carried away at times."

"Well, you might be Jennifer but I am not Jonathan. I'm Marcus. We are not married and we are not amateur detectives. Jenna, we are agents. You have had the training. Just because you have been pushing paper for a year with no real assignment doesn't mean you aren't an agent. Now back to our recap. What did you learn about the Gambionis on the tour today? Oh, one other thing. I also learned that the local office has become aware that all is not well between the cartels in Colombia. Initially, when the small ones were established, they divided up the pie but there now appears to be some squabbling between some of them as to who gets what parts of the operation. Now back to you, what did you learn today."

Angelina had gone to the ship's theatre with Sal, leaving the Gambionis alone in the suite also recapping their day.

"Franco, do we have any family in Sicily?"

"What brought that about? Who's asking?"

"Franco, don't get upset. I was just curious. I never heard you mention anything about them or your father before he passed. I was asked about it today."

"By who? Where?"

"Our tour guide from the ship is from Sicily. She just asked when I told her we were of Sicilian descent. No big deal!"

Franco was getting red in the face and his angry voice was flustering Adriana. "Adriana, this is dangerous territory. Our family ties to Sicily are never discussed and your lack of awareness is intentional. It can put your life in danger. There is a Mafioso capo di tutti in Sicily."

As Franco was speaking, Adriana's thoughts returned to what she heard from the tour guide. *'There is always a family tie.' Was she referring to the mafia?*

Franco continued, "He is the boss of bosses and was arrested a few years ago and is in a prison in Northern Italy but still runs the show. He has had syndicates combined and bosses disappear, including families. He can be ruthless." Color drained from Adriana's face.

"This tour guide. Is she still onboard or did she stay in St. Thomas?" asked Franco.

"She is onboard; she is part of the cruise staff."

"Show her to me tomorrow."

CHAPTER 4

At Sea Again

Marcus had become quite comfortable sharing the cabin with Jenna. As she predicted, it was no different than when he had shared a room with his sister at home. He had given up the foldaway in the sitting room for the other twin bed and luckily neither appeared to snore, so sleep was not a problem. Jenna appeared to sleep the soundest in the morning, so Marcus had no problem getting up and out to the fitness center without waking her. They began to develop a morning routine. Marcus would rise early, go to the fitness center, give Jenna a wakeup call when he was finished and meet for breakfast at the Windows Court. With the Fitness Center being forward, the Windows Court being aft, and their cabin directly below, it was a tossup as to who arrived first. This morning they both went through the food line together and as they settled at a table by the Calypso Pool, they were surprised to see Myla approaching.

"Oh, Oh, we must be on the captain's list this morning," said Jenna. "I wonder what the issue is."

Before Marcus could respond, Myla was at the table. "Good morning, 'newlyweds.' Enjoying the beautiful Caribbean weather this morning?"

"To be sure," responded Marcus, "what's up? I am sure this is not a social call."

"Well, no. You both are invited for coffee with the captain in his cabin at precisely 1000 hours. Please be prompt as this will be followed with a meeting with some additional staff at 1100 hours."

"What staff?" responded Marcus, immediately sensing the possibility of their cover being exposed.

"We have a new issue onboard and I think it best that Captain Hempsell go over it with you himself. See you then." And with that, Myla was gone.

"What could this be all about? We solved the stowaway issue in St. Thomas." said Jenna.

"I am not sure. Howard did mention that they were bringing new crew onboard yesterday but I don't see how that could be an issue. They do that all the time. Look, we better hustle; I have to clean up before we go."

———— ·•·— ————

Captain Hempsell's cabin included a roomy sitting area with a large coffee table. To both Jenna and Marcus's delight, it was adorned with not only a coffee and tea service but a large basket of English crumpets and scones. Butter, marmalade, and Devonshire cream allowed for a gratifying mid-morning snack.

"Captain, I would have to double my visits to the fitness center if I indulged in this every morning," said Marcus.

"It's only for my guests," said the captain. "I prefer tea with milk only mid-morning. But please, be my guest." Then, in a serious tone he continued, "I brought you here early to advise you of some issues that could affect your assignment and maybe your cover. It may surprise you as it did me, but we have an Interpol agent onboard and it turns out she is also on my staff. She will be joining us shortly and will better explain the issues I refer to."

———— ·•·— ————

Marcus was applying marmalade and Devonshire cream to

his third scone as Security Officer Smith arrived with an attractive dark-haired female staff member in tow. Jenna jumped up from the table, almost knocking over the tea service and with a questioning cry said, "Martina? An Interpol agent? I can't believe it!"

Captain Hempsell immediately responded to all, "May I introduce you to Agent Martina Bufalino, Interpol. She joined our staff in Halifax as a very competent shore excursion tour guide. I was totally unaware that she was undercover."

"I apologize again, Captain. This was arranged through Duchess Headquarters and I just assumed they would have informed you and Security Officer Smith."

"There was a major staff change in Halifax and communication with Duchess HR is not always the greatest. That's not really an issue. Now if I may," said the captain, pausing and looking at Marcus who immediately shook his head yes, "Introduce CIA Agents Peterson and Adams. I believe we have issues that involve your assignments as well as my ship. Agent Bufalino, would you please recap what you reported to me earlier?"

"Martina, please, sir," said Agent Bufalino. Then looking at Jenna she asked, "You are not married?"

Marcus quickly responded, "You have your cover, we have ours. Please continue."

Martina went into a detailed dialog on how Italian security agencies became aware of the Sicilian Cosa Nostra endeavoring to reestablish ties to the Mafia families in the US, specifically related to the drug trade.

"The FBI and your agency both made Interpol aware of the Gambioni planned trip as they anticipated an Italian connection might be established while Franco was out of the country." said Martina.

"This was never passed on to us," interrupted Marcus.

"That's probably because Interpol did not initially anticipate sending an agent. In fact, I wouldn't be surprised if they still have not informed either the FBI or the CIA that I was dispatched. You have your bureaucratic problems. We have ours. Now my assignment is to establish if any Italian contact is made. And yours?"

Jenna jumped into the conversation, "Our primary mission is to track the possible establishment of a connection of the Gambioni family with a Colombian drug cartel. To date, we believe a meeting is being set up with Pablo Londoño, but our agency just informed us locally that there appear to be issues between the cartels in Colombia and one or more other cartels may be trying to usurp any Londoño/Gambioni deal before it's established."

Almost simultaneously Marcus and Martina looked at Captain Hempsell and said,

"Captain, how does this affect your ship?"

"I am not sure you are aware, but we made a sizeable staff change in St. Thomas. In fact, we held up sailing awaiting a delayed flight from Italy. Our new executive chef arrived on that plane. However, that flight included several other staff members either recruited or returning. As with Martina, there would be no indication in their personnel records if any had Mafia connections." Then looking at Marcus and Jenna, he continued, "By the way, we also put on several staff from South America. I am not sure from which country."

Security Officer Smith jumped into the conversation, "Sir, I have checked their records. All appear to have Venezuelan passports. However, that would not preclude any from being a part of a Colombian cartel. There is a pretty soft border between those countries."

"Let me see if I can summarize," said Marcus. "Known facts. We have the Gambioni family onboard. They have made contact with the Londoño drug cartel. Period. That's really all we know for sure."

All attention was given to Marcus. Jenna appeared busy buttering another scone, Martina taking notes on a napkin, Security

Officer Smith shuffling through the papers he brought with him. Captain Hempsell said, "Marcus, please continue."

"Speculation. First, a Sicilian Mafia/Gambioni family contact is anticipated. Whether it will be onboard or in a port is unknown. Whether it will be friendly or hostile is also unknown. Second, a competing Colombian cartel may enter the picture. When, how and who is also an unknown."

"Marcus," interrupted the captain, "did your agency have any further definition as whether these cartel squabbles were serious and which ones were in the frenzy? I am not sure how that affects the surveillance of the Gambioni family."

"No, they did not. They indicated this was reported by operatives they had in-country and at this juncture it was not clear whether it was only talk or action," responded Marcus.

All eyes immediately focused on Martina as she set her coffee cup down with force and exclaimed, "Oh, my God. It never occurred to me. We are well aware of the Sicilian Mafia getting drugs directly from Colombia. The cartel they are dealing with could well be different and a competitor of the Londoño cartel. This could get really complicated."

———•◆•———

"Father, I am sure you are overreacting," said Angelina as they approached the Shore Excursion desk on deck 7. From the expression on both their faces it was obvious that this was a serious dialog.

"Angelina, no more. Just show me this Italian excursion person or whatever you call her."

At the desk, Angelina asked for Martina and was told that she was unavailable at the moment but could be reached in the Duchess Theatre at noon where she would be giving a shore excursion talk on Aruba, the next port.

Overhearing this, Franco exclaimed in a somewhat loud voice, "Angelina, we will go there and you will introduce me."

"Father, please don't make a public scene. I am still sure it was just a friendly question."

"We will see." And with that Franco stormed off, leaving Angelina apologizing to the staff person on duty for her father's abruptness.

———•———

It was English Pub night in the Portofino Dining Room. The serving staff were in their red, white and blue striped vests with red bow ties. However, they appeared to be somewhat disorganized at the station serving the Gambioni table. It was obvious that there had been some personnel changes and waiters were having trouble with the indoctrination of new help who had joined the ship in St. Thomas. Above the noise of dishes being stacked on the waiter's stations came, "Rizzo, what are you doing? Where did you learn to be a waiter?" It was the lead waiter at the station serving the Gambionis.

The help they send us these days from Italy is atrocious, not at all up to the standards of the past, thought the lead waiter. *Now what is he trying to do?* "Rizzo! Here!"

Rizzo, walking back to the waiters' station, thought, *I have got to warn Franco Gambioni of the contact that will occur in Aruba. This waiter's job is the pits; I just can't believe some of the assignments I get, but the Sicilian Mafioso pays me well and takes care of my family. I guess I shouldn't complain.*

Speaking to the lead waiter, he said, "I'm sorry. I was just going to ask the guests how they were enjoying the meal."

———•———

The next morning at the Windows Court found Rizzo not very happy having to work the dining room until closing and then be up at the crack of dawn to work the Windows Court. Again he thought, *This job is the pits.* But the situation quickly improved as he spotted Adriana and Franco in one of the buffet lines. *Ah, at last an opportunity to warn Franco,* he thought.

But before he could approach them, he was summoned to the kitchen. *Porca vacca, I have got to warn Franco before we arrive in Aruba,* he thought.

"Rizzo, report to the spa. The juice bars have to be set up for the day," commanded the head waiter.

Merda, I'll never get to the Gambioni family.

In the Fitness Center, Marcus finished his aerobic routine on the treadmill, and slipped on a sweat shirt and headed to the Body Oasis Spa. *Just maybe I'll see Angelina again in the spa,* he thought.

The steam room had stone chairs on three sides and a stone platform extending back into an unlighted section of the room. One could be lying on the platform and not be noticed by anyone entering or sitting in the forward area. Marcus came in, laid his towel down and sat on the end of the platform facing the lighted area of the room. The perspiration started to drip off his arms and legs and he glanced down at the wet floor.

"Holy shit," he exclaimed out loud, "that's got to be blood."

Security Officer Smith identified the body as Rizzo Sebastiani, an Italian waiter who came on board at St. Thomas. The cause of death appeared to be a severe blow to the neck causing a crushing of the trachea resulting in immediate loss of air and hemorrhaging from the mouth. This would have to be verified by a coroner. Marcus explained that no one else appeared to be in the spa when he arrived, but with three separate steam rooms adjoining the main pool and shower area, there was no assurance that that was true.

They were again assembled in Captain Hempsell's office:

Marcus, Jenna, Martina, Captain Hempsell and Security Officer Smith. "We certainly have experienced death on our ships but never to my knowledge a murder," said the captain. "I have ordered the spa closed and the body has been transferred to the morgue," he continued. Then seeing the surprised expressions on Jenna, Marcus, and Marina's faces, he said, "Yes, we do have a morgue. It can hold up to three bodies. As you are probably aware, many of our passengers are seniors and unfortunately it is not uncommon for us to lose one to a heart attack, a serious fall, or what have you. When that happens we usually try to disembark the body in the country of origin, i.e. the US. Now we do have a bit of a dilemma. We have what appears to be a murder, no knowledge of a motive, and the murderer could be anywhere on board, within the population of passengers and/or crew."

"I might be able to shed some light on the motive," said Martina. "I have emailed Interpol headquarters in Italy and they are researching the name Rizzo Sebastiani as we speak. He may be a member of the Sicilian Mafioso that is doing business with a Colombian drug cartel. Their response could shed some light on the situation."

"If he is, who would want to kill him?" asked Marcus. "I doubt it could be the Londoño cartel as we are aware that their potential hit man is not on board. We saw him in St. Thomas on board the Londoño yacht."

"That's a question we surely do not have an answer to," said Security Officer Smith. "My question is what I tell customs and security in Aruba before or when we arrive. I'm not sure how they will react to me telling them I have a murderer somewhere on board the ship. Captain, have you spoken to fleet headquarters? Did they give you any guidance?"

"Yes, and you're probably not going to believe this. Their response is: find the murderer before you dock, turn all over to Aruba authorities, avoid all publicity, and maintain your schedule. We must avoid any possibilities of passenger unrest that could result in lawsuits against the company."

"You have got to be kidding," said Jenna. "They obviously have no concept of the situation we are dealing with here."

Looking at Security Officer Smith the captain said, "I suggest you go through all of Sebastiani's possessions to see if there's any clue as to what he was doing on board beside being a waiter and also question the food service staff to see what his assignments were and see if they can shed any light as to his friends on board and/or potential enemies. He has only been onboard a day and a half so you might not learn much. Marcus, Jenna, could you accompany me to the bridge? We can review the security camera recordings in the area of the spa. They may show who was in the area around the time that you were and before. Unfortunately, the cameras in the spa get fogged up at times but the ones in the passageway should be good."

Looking at everyone else in the room, he said, "Let's get back here in a couple of hours and share whatever information we collectively come up with. Thank you."

With that, everyone left the captain's cabin and went their way.

———•◆•———

As they entered the cabin, Jenna threw her arms around Marcus, giving him a passionate kiss and saying, "Can you believe it? We resolved the crime in less than four hours. We are amazing. We are a formidable team."

"Now hold on," said Marcus. "There were a few others involved. Like the captain, Security Officer Smith, and Interpol Agent Bufalino. But you're right, it was exciting. I'm sure the culprit didn't realize there are security cameras all over the ship. And he obviously had not had time to get rid of the bloodstained sneakers he had on. It amazed me how quickly Security Officer Smith was able to apprehend him when we identified him on the security camera stream.

I wonder what the authorities will do in Aruba. The victim was an Italian, the suspected murderer carries a Venezuelan passport and the murder occurred on board a ship at sea."

"I don't know, but we have our own issues to deal with in Aruba. I'm not sure how we do it, but we've got to keep an eye on the whole Gambioni family. We've got to try to identify who makes what contacts with whom." said Jenna.

"Well, we better get ready. We cannot be late. We have been invited to sit with the Gambioni family and Sal for dinner. I have no idea what that's all about but I'm sure we will find out. And Marcus, remember we are newlyweds. Watch the Angelina ogling."

———•◆•———

The Gambioni family had a unique table. It was one of the few oval tables in the dining room. It provided a little closer contact for easy conversation. Marcus and Jenna were seated opposite at one of the narrow ends of the table and Franco and Adriano at the other with Sal and Angelina opposite each other in the center. The meal had been ordered, the wine poured, (with the exception of Sal who claimed he didn't drink while on duty) and Franco raised his glass, saying, "*Cin Cin.*" Angelina immediately countered, "No, no, Father. *Salute.* We are all friends."

"*Si,* Angelina, *salute,*" responded Franco. As the glasses clinked and came down, the table erupted into individual conversations with Marcus talking to Angelina next to him and Jenna speaking to Sal next to her. As the discussions continued, Marcus felt Jenna's foot slowly rubbing his leg, which he had extended in front of him under the table. She had obviously removed her shoe and continued looking directly at Sal paying no attention to the conversation going on between him and Angelina.

What is going on here? he thought. *First the passionate kiss when we returned to the room and now this. Is this her version of the newlywed game or is it for real?* he asked himself.

"Marcus, are you listening to me?" Angelina asked, "You're looking at me but appear to be in another world."

"Oh I'm sorry," said Marcus "I guess I am still a little distraught from what happened this morning."

"What do you mean? What happened?" asked Angelina.

With that question all table conversation ceased and all eyes turned to Marcus. *Oh, shit,* thought Jenna, *he's going to blow our cover.*

"Well, I don't want to disturb anybody but you wouldn't believe what happened," Marcus continued.

<hr />

After a fascinating dinner involving compelling conversation and followed by entertainment and dancing at the Bridge Bar with Angelina and Sal, Marcus and Jenna returned to their stateroom and followed what had become their normal routine. Marcus had first turn in the closet dressing area and bathroom while Jenna sat at the vanity/desk removing her shoes and jewelry.

"That was an interesting story you told about this morning's adventure. I was sure you were going to give away our cover when you started," called out Jenna.

Marcus, returning in his pajamas and retiring to the couch to read the Patter that somehow always appeared in their mailbox before they returned in the evening, responded, "I thought you would like it. I just wanted to make the Gambionis and Sal aware that something did happen that could affect them without telling the real story."

As Jenna retired to the dressing area and Marcus looked at the Patter, he was surprised to read the announcement that the spa would be closed indefinitely due to facility issues. He called to Jenna, saying, "You are not going to believe this but what I experienced this morning and related at dinner in a fabricated story is being depicted to the passengers as a facility issue. I would say that's a bit of an understatement."

So engrossed in his reading, he was not immediately aware that Jenna had emerged from the dressing area, but he quickly looked up when she responded in a low throaty voice, "You make a far better story teller."

He was totally taken back, it was happening so fast; her low voice, a provocative scent, and her approaching him dressed in a very revealing negligee. She was not wearing a nightgown and the soft filmy fabric of the negligee left little to the imagination. He suddenly became aware of a Jenna he had not been conscious of before. Seeing her voluptuous body captivated his attention, immediately arousing him. Before he could utter a word, she was there pulling him up from the couch, her negligee falling open as she pressed her body against him and her lips to his mouth in a passionate kiss. The heat of desire clouded their consciousness as they fell back on the couch and their bodies entangled in a sexual embrace. Their lovemaking was repeated in his bed, though Marcus was not aware of how they got there. Following multiple intimate relations, they fell fast asleep, bodies entwined. Waking, Marcus looked at Jenna, still asleep next to him, and now saw a beautiful female, erasing any thoughts of an Angelina from his mind and replacing them with only those of the woman next to him.

Jenna opened her eyes and with a soft smile looking at Marcus said, "Hi."

CHAPTER 5

Aruba

It was a little past noon when the Reina del Mar docked in Aruba. The weather had been perfect for the trip. With calm seas and mild winds, she made the 500-plus mile trip in a little over 21 hours. Though the yacht had a top speed of 28 knots, Señora Londoño had ordered she be run at the cruising speed of 24 to conserve fuel. The señora had spent much of the night on the radio with Pablo discussing the Gambioni meeting as well as how operations were going in the country. She had not put her head down until early dawn so the crew hesitated to wake her when they were finally tied up at the assigned dock in the Oranjestad harbor.

Alphonse Romano looked out of place standing on the wharf in a dark business suit. He had checked with Aruba Port Control and was told that the Reina del Mar had radioed ahead and was directed to berth at the wharf just north of the cruise ship dock. The Port Captain walked him out to the end of the pier and pointed the yacht out as it had just cleared the breakwater and was heading into the harbor area. Franco had not given Alphonse a time. His instructions were to be at the dock when the yacht arrived and meet with Señora Londoño. He therefore had come directly from the airport to be sure he was on time as expected. This was not as easy as he thought. Not knowing that Aruba was a part of the Netherlands, he was a little put off when getting into the cab and the driver greeted him in Dutch. He soon found the driver also spoke English but only as a second language so he had a little difficulty explaining his need to get to the port area as opposed to somewhere in town.

Standing there alone, his thoughts were, *How lucky is that. Franco said he would guess that the Londoño yacht would arrive at midday and all I could do was book the earliest flight available and hope it coincided and it did.*

Ricardo was on deck and had spotted the lone greeter as they motored to their assigned berth. "Welcome to Aruba, Señor. You are Señor Romano?" he called out as the last lines were secured.

"Yes," responded Alphonse. "Is Señora Londoño available? I am supposed to meet with her."

"*Si*, Señor, but not for another hour and not here. If you look behind, you will see two officials walking toward us on the pier. I believe they are Aruba Immigration and Customs officials and they will have to clear us before we are allowed on shore or you are allowed on board. As soon as we are cleared, the Reina del Mar will proceed to the Renaissance Marina, which I believe you passed on your way in from the airport. I suggest we meet there. It's a relatively small marina so I am sure you will be able to see our location when we arrive. *Adios*, Señor."

And with that, Ricardo turned to the Aruba officials and helped them aboard.

——— · ———

Alphonse was halfway out the quay to the Reina del Mar when he spotted Ricardo coming toward him accompanied by an extremely attractive dark-haired woman. *That must be Señora Londoño*, he thought. *What a looker. This could be an interesting meeting.*

As they came closer, she called out, "Señor Romano, I am

Señora Londoño. Welcome to Aruba." She extended her hand as they met.

"Señora, my pleasure," responded Alphonse, shaking her hand.

"You have met Ricardo earlier, I believe," she said, nodding in Ricardo's direction. Without waiting for a response, she continued, "We will meet on shore. My boat needs refueling and I have a favorite place for breakfast close by. It's the only place open at this early hour. Come, it's a short, easy walk," the señora said as she proceeded to lead them off the dock.

This could be an interesting discussion, thought Alphonse. *From her thick Spanish accent, it's obvious that English is not her first language.*

They proceeded a short way down L.G. Smith Boulevard and went into The Dutch Pancake House.

"Señora Londoño, welcome back," said the maître d' as they entered. "You have been missed. Come, your table is waiting."

Following the maître d' to a somewhat secluded table, Alphonse remarked, "You are known here."

"*Si,* we often stop here when returning to Cartagena," responded the señora. As they were seated, the señora continued, "Señor Romano, I received some disturbing news last night from my husband. You may not be aware that another Colombian cartel does business with the Mafia in Sicily. We understand that they are aware of Franco's desire to enhance his US drug trade with our products and they are not totally pleased of not being a part of the action. We further became aware that the Mafia may be sending an emissary to convince Franco to do business through them and their cartel. Their methods of persuasion could be dangerous. I would suggest you warn your boss when he arrives tomorrow. Now, let us sit down and discuss the details of our proposed arrangement that I believe we both would like to put in place. Assuming we can come to some agreement, Pablo's meeting with your boss in Cartagena could be very productive for both organizations."

"Señora, I thought you would be meeting with Franco again tomorrow when the Golden Duchess arrives."

"No, señor. Our meeting in St. Thomas was sufficient. You and I are to discuss how we envision the operation working. If we have agreement on the details, I will proceed to Cartagena to arrange the meeting between Pablo and Señor Gambioni. Be assured, I will personally meet the ship in Cartagena and escort Señor Gambioni to the meeting place."

As they sat down to proceed with the discussion on the logistics of drug transfer, Alphonse's mind went into overdrive. *I wonder if Franco has been contacted. He certainly didn't tell me on our phone conversation. This could get real messy if Sicily is involved, and who is this other cartel? Is the Gambioni family in danger? I hope that his security team is watching out for them.*

"Señor, Señor. Are you alright?" said Señora Londoño.

"Oh, sorry, Señora, I was in deep thought about the information you passed on. Now, about the product movement. Our family pretty much controls the docks in Brooklyn," responded Alphonse as his consciousness came back to the discussion he was having with the señora.

———•◆•———

Though it had been announced by the navigator during yesterday's noon watch report and published in the Patter last night that the arrival would be at 7 am, the Golden Duchess 's final lines were secured at the cruise ship dock in Aruba at 5:45 am. Most all passengers were still asleep. A long black hearse and two police ATVs were parked about amidships on the wharf, their engines running. The piercing ring of the cabin phone shattered the tranquil mood of the new lovers in the Peterson cabin. Marcus leaped out of bed and ran to the phone near Jenna's bed on the other side of the cabin. "Yes, Marcus here," he answered.

"Good morning, this is Security Officer Smith. I suggest you go out on your balcony and view the operation. Later!" and with that the phone went dead.

Jenna ran to the bathroom for their robes, thoughts racing through her mind. *Was I wrong to seduce Marcus? I do have feelings for him. I was hoping he would really see me.*

"Quick, Jenna," Marcus called out as he opened the door to the balcony. The fugitive transfer is about to take place. The passenger gangways had not yet been installed but through the shell door on Deck Four and a temporary ramp, Security Officer Smith and the ship's security personnel appeared, escorting the hand-cuffed prisoner off the ship and turning him over to the Korps Politie Aruba or KPA. Immediately following, a wooden casket appeared on a gurney being wheeled to the waiting hearse.

As the ATVs and the hearse drove off, Marcus said, "Have you ever seen such an efficient operation? It all took less than 15 or 20 minutes. Most passengers will never know what happened."

"Yeah, the NYPD could learn something watching this operation," said Jenna. "I wonder what will happen to the accused assailant."

"We will have to check with Security Officer Smith later in the day. I'm sure he will have a story to tell."

With that said, they went back inside to prepare for the day. Jenna's immediate thought was, *Please Marcus, say something about last night.*

———————

Jenna, filled with anticipation and joy as she led the small group from the chartered van through the palm-lined walk to the beach, was pleasantly rewarded to find Palm Beach exactly as she remembered from when she had been brought here by her parents. The walkway ended at a pathway to a pier and a beach walkway going in both directions. The pier provided a home for the local watering hole for beach goers and shops trafficking swimwear and souvenirs. Hotels bordered the beach walkway in both directions. Jenna turned right, leading her troupe to the Radisson Aruba Caribbean Resort. Its location provided a back-drop to a beautiful wide beach with palm trees and thatched palm shade umbrellas randomly scattered on the sand between the walkway along the resort grounds edge and the water. They were large enough to provide shade for two or more lounge chairs and had small tables fastened around their base. Some were arranged in clusters to accommodate small groups. The sand appeared almost sugar white and was fine and easily squished between the toes as you walked on it. Sal, having gone out ahead of the group to check the security of the area, had already selected a space he felt provided him an environment in which he could best protect his charges. It was close to the water's edge and a good distance from the beach walkway. He waved to Jenna as she came with the group.

The outing had turned into a mini shore excursion. Martina, having befriended Adriana, had joined the group and after meet-ing with her earlier, Franco had satisfied himself that she was no more than what she professed to be.

Marcus and Jenna picked a spot close to the Gambionis but just enough distance away that casual conversation would not be overheard. As they spread their towels on the lounge chairs, Jenna said in a low voice to Marcus, "It appears that things have settled down in the Gambioni family. I could not believe what we witnessed this morning when disembarking and Adriana spot-ted that man she called Alphonse walking up to greet Franco."

"I know," said Marcus, "I don't understand Italian but it was obvious she was giving Franco one large chewing out. And it got louder when he and Alphonse walked away to talk in private."

"Well, it appears all is well for now," said Jenna and then, with a grin appearing on her face, she continued, "I wonder what Franco would think if he realized he was in the company of two CIA agents and an Interpol agent?"

"Careful, Jenna, we don't want the cover blown," said Marcus and then, starting toward the water, in a loud voice he called out, "Angelina, Sal, last one in the water gets the drinks."

As the four ran toward the water, Martina said, "Adriana, did you spot that shop of local beach clothes we passed as we walked in? Come. Let's explore."

As they all went off in different directions, leaving Franco to mind their belongings, no one noticed the stranger dressed in a white palm beach suit wearing a Panama hat. He watched them settle in and then approached Franco.

———•—•———

Howard Smith, a retired detective from the Los Angeles Sheriff's Department, never dreamed of how complicated his new retirement job would become. He had envisioned that a security officer on a cruise ship would be an outstanding follow-on after spending so many years fighting crime in LA. He would be able to take his wife to places he could never afford before. What a great opportunity. His qualifications more than exceeded what the cruise line required. Well, it was turning out to be a far cry from what he had anticipated.

After his indoctrination, he remembered those final words uttered by his new cruise line boss. "Now remember, shipboard crime is bad publicity for a cruise line. It must be prevented if at all possible and never publicized. Addressing crime will be no different than your past career. Those that perpetrate crime must be dealt with according to the law. Oh, and finally, at sea, the captain of the ship is the final word on any situation."

That advice all sounded pretty straightforward at the time. It wasn't until later that he realized that that part about according to the law was a little more complicated than he thought. It all depended on where the ship was when the crime occurred and who was involved. At the time, he never dreamed he would be dealing with a murder. A robbery or assault possibly, nothing more serious. How wrong he was.

Shortly after docking, he and Martina were on a conference call to Interpol in Sicily. Due to the time difference it was already close to eleven o'clock in Italy and close to the time that the Interpol office would be closed for the scheduled three-hour break at noon. The officer they spoke to indicated that it had been verified that the recruiting agency responsible for hiring and vetting new employees for the cruise line had accommodated a Sicilian Mafia request to hire Rizzo Sebastiani for the cruise line and vet him as a responsible law-abiding employee. Due to the nature of his employment, Interpol suggested that the body be sent back to his family of record. Further, they doubted whether any inquiry as to cause of death would occur. Following the call, Security Officer Smith went immediately to Captain Hempsell's office. In his haste he entered the office without knocking and found the captain on the phone with cruise line headquarters.

"Sorry, sir," he said quietly and Captain Hempsell motioned him to sit.

"Yes, sir, I completely understand. We will do our best to follow that scenario and if any difficulty occurs, I will inform you immediately," said Captain Hempsell on the phone. After a short pause, he continued, "Yes, I am afraid the two issues could be connected. I will instruct the CIA agents of our policy and make them aware of the maritime law." And with that said, he finished the call and addressed Security Officer Smith. "That was the Commodore/Director of Operations. We have our orders. Since no Americans are involved and we are in international waters, we are not required to inform the FBI. They wish us to place the issue entirely in the hands of the local authorities if at all possible. It is felt that Aruba authorities will be just as interested in keeping this from the press as we are due to the possible impact on their tourist trade."

Security Officer Smith then explained what he had learned from the Interpol telecon.

"Our local agent will be meeting me at the mortuary and will be able to follow through on the body shipment. I will explain to him our current company position on the entire issue."

"After that, I assume you plan to go to KPA headquarters?"

"Yes, sir. I am not sure how Aruba authorities will want to deal with the assailant. Their response to me this morning when they took possession was that I would have to file charges for him to be held or describe how he violated Aruba law."

"Welcome to the frustrations of international law. Go do what you have to but try to keep the cruise line out of it, if at all possible."

With that said, Security Officer Smith left and was on his mission.

———

The local mortuary was almost in walking distance from the ship. However, arrangements for the body shipment began to involve more time than Security Officer Smith could provide. The local cruise line port agent assured him he would take care of the details so Smith was off in a taxi on his way to Santa Cruz and KPA headquarters. As the cab was speeding along the 5A highway to Santa Cruz, Smith had time to reflect on the past few hours and his thoughts were a mental dialog of what had happened and what he must accomplish and how.

If a murder occurred, the local authorities will want to see the body. I have pictures of the crime scene, but I'm sure they will still want to see the body. Now the surveillance films that we used to catch the assailant could be a problem. I can't provide them with copies as company policy forbids it. But we do have his blood-stained clothes and when first accosted, he admitted to killing Rizzo. That should be enough. I really don't know much about Aruba law. I don't even know if they have a death penalty. His thought pattern was shattered when the cab came to a halt and the cab driver shouted out, "Twenty dollars American."

The KPA officers he had turned the assailant over to in the morning met him at the door. It appeared they had been waiting for him. After signing him in, they escorted him to the confinement area where he acknowledged that the prisoner being held was the one he had turned over. They then took him to the Deputy Commissioner's office, wished him luck and left.

On entering the office, Smith was surprised to see a man that he thought by all appearances, uniform, physical attributes, and welcoming voice resembled a Nazi Gestapo officer he had seen in an old World War II movie. He proceeded to tell his story of what had happened onboard and was again put off guard when interrupted.

"Look, Officer Smith," said the Commissioner in a very commanding voice. "The captive you turned over to us has not committed a crime in Aruba. He claims he has committed no crime at all. You have claimed he committed a murder aboard your ship but there appear to be no witnesses to testify to this. You have provided us with pictures of the so-called crime scene but again no verification that the accused assailant was present. You claim you have surveillance camera data showing the assailant leaving the proximity of the murder but can't provide a copy."

"The victim's body can be viewed at the mortuary in Oranjestad," interrupted Smith.

"That's of no matter. The accused also claims to be employed by you."

"That is correct."

"As I said initially, the detainee has not broken any Aruba law and you have filed no charges, so the best the KPA can do is return the so-called assailant to Venezuelan authorities, his home country listed on his passport. You should press any charges you wish in that country to justify his custody. Your cruise line will be billed any and all expenses associated with that exercise. In addition, this will not be mentioned to the media because nothing has really happened here in Aruba."

Smith could not believe the total lack of jurisprudence he had just experienced.

CHAPTER 6

Aruba Waters

Marcus

The wakeup call by Smith and witnessing the prisoner transfer put Marcus's mind in total focus on their primary assignment. He was sure contact would be made with Franco on this outing. Though Jenna had picked the location, he knew that Sal would set up some security, possibly using his partner who mostly remained distant from the Gambioni family gatherings. His mind had been in a spin since they hit the beach. As he stripped down to his swim suit, he thought, *There is no way Sal will anticipate that there are other factions that wish to contact Franco. I feel so powerless. I know I can't, but I feel I should tell Sal about the Sicilian Mafia, the competing drug cartel, the murder we experienced. Hell, I've got to clear my mind.*

Picking up the beach ball they had brought along, he ran toward the water and yelled to the others. Sal was right behind him and they both hit the water together. The initial water contact cleared his head. He threw the ball to Sal and started swimming. Several strokes out he realized it was still fairly shallow, so standing on the bottom, he gazed back at the beach. Angelina in her yellow polka dot bikini immediately caught his attention as both girls raced to the water and she called out as she hit the first wave. He called back to her and then focused on Jenna, also in a bikini. His thoughts flashed back to last night. *Two years working together. How did I never notice?* he thought.

Jenna

At Marcus's challenge Jenna dropped her cover-up on the chaise lounge and raced toward the water with the others. The sand was soft at first, inhibiting her gait, but as she approached the hardened sand near the water's edge, she picked up speed. Marcus and Sal had already entered the water and even though Angelina had started before her, Jenna's thoughts were, *You're not going to beat me, you prissy bitch.* Her jealousy was erupting from her subconscious.

It was difficult to tell who made it first, as a small swell hit the beach as they both entered the water. "Ow, it's cold," screamed Angelina.

"It's fine after you get wet," called out Marcus.

Jenna never felt the water temperature as her total mind set was on Marcus and his obvious continued infatuation with Angelina. *Damn,* she thought, *was last night all forgotten.* Her thoughts were shattered as the beach ball came toward her and Sal called out, "In your face, Jenna."

Sal

For the first time on the trip, Sal felt he had everything under control. Here he was about to spend some glorious time on a fabulous beach in the company of two extremely attractive women. Thoughts raced through his mind as he watched the girls run into the water. *What a great job this has turned out to be. From the discussion with Alphonse this morning, all seems to be set in motion for the Gambioni / Londoño meeting in Cartagena. There shouldn't be any security issues until we get there. Franco appears to be relaxed, and it's apparent he has made peace with Adriana, at least until we get to Cartagena. This is so . . .*

"Here," called Marcus as he threw the beach ball at Sal, shattering Sal's thought process.

Catching the ball, Sal spotted Jenna first and threw it to her. Then his eyes caught Angelina.

Wow. What a body, he thought. *That could tempt me to give up my business rule. 'Don't get involved with the customer.'*

It was on the third go-around with the beach ball that he happened to looked up on shore and froze with panic. No one was in the vicinity of their belongings. Franco was gone.

Martina

As she and Adriana walked towards the pier, they engaged in Italian small talk. Her thoughts, however, were of how she had befriended herself into the Gambioni family. *I really have to pride myself at winning over Franco's trust,* she thought. *I am sure he thought I was Mafia. If he knew I was Interpol, he would die,* she chuckled to herself.

Switching to English, she said, "Let's go into this first shop. It had some great cover-ups I saw on my last trip." A definite lie, but again uttered to further gain acceptance as a friendly expert.

As they entered the shop and started looking through the ever-present rack of clothes that had the usual On Sale sign, Martina shuddered. It was her sixth scent that told her something was not right. Looking around, she realized they were totally alone in the shop. "Adriana, come" she said, grabbing her hand and almost forcing Adriana toward the door.

"What, what's the matter," cried Adriana.

"It may be nothing," responded Martina, "but I don't like being in a shop in a foreign country without the purveyor present. It has the potential of putting you in a very difficult position."

Rushing out the door, Martina bumped into a portly woman in a flowered sarong, almost knocking her off the pier into the sand. "Forgive me," she said.

Catching her balance the woman responded, "That's quite alright, I am the shop keeper. May I help you?"

"Maybe later," said Martina.

"Please, I have some beautiful things. Come back in," said the shopkeeper.

"I'm sorry, we must leave right now but we will be back," said Martina.

"Yes, we will," added Adriana, and as they scurried off the pier into the sand, she said to Martina, "I had no idea we would be actually buying anything, I have to get some money from Franco and come back. I spotted something I really liked."

Partway down the walkway toward the Radisson, they both stopped looking ahead and said almost simultaneously, "Something is wrong. Where is Franco?"

"*Benvenuto*, Franco Gambioni. I bring greetings from the *capo di tutti*." The words were spoken in Sicilian Italian immediately recognizable by Franco and it sent chills down his back as he turned around to see who was speaking. "The *capo* hopes you are enjoying your cruise vacation," the stranger continued.

Franco's mind went into a spin. *Our family has never had an issue with the* capo di tutti. *In fact, none of the Mafia families in the New York area have experienced any dealings with Sicilian Cosa Nostra for over a generation*, he thought. *Whoever this individual is, he is attempting to violate this first and cardinal rule of the Mafia. If he is real, he should know there must always be a third party known to both to make any introduction.*

Looking over the shoulder of the well-dressed man in front of him, he spotted Sal's assistant sitting on a bench on the beach walk no more than 30 feet away. He nodded and Franco nodded back. This eased the tension a little but Franco still had major concerns.

"Come, let's share a libation. We have a mutual friend waiting," the stranger continued, pointing to Gilligan's, the Radisson Beach bar restaurant just a short ways up the beach walk.

What mutual friend could we have? thought Franco. *Mutual friend? Maybe this guy is for real.*

He nodded again toward Sal's assistant and proceeded to follow the stranger who had started walking towards the outside bar. As they got closer to the restaurant, Franco spotted Alphonse sitting at one of the outside tables. He immediately became a little more relieved but was now filled with curiosity. *How does Alphonse know this guy?* he wondered.

As they approached the table, Alphonse got up and said, "Franco, let me introduce you to Luciano Guerra from Palermo. I met him on one of my trips to Sicily. He is one of us."

Franco, hearing the magic words, "he is one of us," eased his demeanor and they all sat down. In Sicilian Italian, Franco said, "Welcome, Luciano, my pleasure. How are things in Palermo?"

Before Luciano could answer, Alphonse in a low voice said to Franco, "I sat up here as I didn't think it would be wise for Adriana to see me."

Following small talk in Italian, the conversation switched to English and Luciano in a polite way informed Franco and Alphonse about the arrangement the Sicilian Mafia had with a Colombian drug cartel. The drug lord of this cartel was not Pablo Londoño and appeared to be an obvious competitor cartel. Luciano continued to explain how happy they were with this current arrangement and ended by suggesting that Franco should seriously consider the same cartel for his family's needs.

Franco was well aware that when Pablo Escobar and the Medellin cartel was dismantled, several of the lieutenants established small cartels continuing the cocaine trade. The Londoño cartel was the only one he was aware of doing business with families in the US. With this suggestion from the Sicilian Mafioso, his thought process went into overdrive. *Is the Sicilian Mafia trying to get back into operations in the US? Is this a suggestion so they get a piece of the action? If I did what they suggested, how would I deal with Londoño? What will be the consequences no matter which way I go?*

Before Franco could respond, Luciano rose and excused himself, saying, "Enjoy the rest of your cruise. We will be in touch."

And with that he was gone.

"Alphonse, who the hell is this guy? What have you gotten us into?" said Franco.

As color began to drain from Alphonse's face, he said, "Franco, I had no idea. It was at a family gathering in Palermo that I met him. I think my cousin introduced him as a close friend of the *capo*. It was a social event. I have heard nothing about him since. Hell, that was over a year ago when I was back there."

"And?" said Franco in a stern voice with eyes piercing Alphonse's face.

"Boss, I told you this morning what Señora Londoño said about the other drug cartel and the Sicily Mafia. Remember, we were interrupted by Adriana and had to break off our discussion. What I didn't have time to tell you was that I stayed at the Renaissance Aruba last night, the one hotel closest to the cruise ship pier and recommended by Señora Londoño. Out of the blue this guy shows up and approaches me at the bar. How he knew I was in Aruba and staying there is beyond me. I tell you, Boss, there has to be more that we don't know."

"This is getting messy," said Franco, his expression becoming more questioning than annoyed.

"Boss, as I told you this morning, everything is set up for your meeting in Cartagena tomorrow with Pablo. I don't know what you do now."

Looking towards the beach Franco spotted the family group coming out of the water and scampering on the hot sand to the area where they had left their belongings. He said to Alphonse, "I must get back; we will talk. Have the waiter bring down a pitcher of rum punch and glasses."

Getting up, Franco rapidly walked back to the area calling to Sal, who appeared to be approaching first, "Hey, Sal, I'm here. I just went up to the bar. Not to worry, your assistant was watching. Drinks for all are on the way."

———•—•———

The rum punch that Franco provided tended to loosen the group up and concerns for his whereabouts slipped from their consciousness. The remaining time at the beach was spent with some water play but mainly soaking up the sun. The chartered limo returned them all to the ship and the plan was to meet at dockside at five o'clock and walk to a restaurant in town that had been recommended to Martina by the crew's staff.

The duvet had been pulled down on the now configured double bed in the Peterson cabin and the unclothed feminine form lying face down on the white sheet resembled a large piece of red coral on a white sandy beach. Marcus carefully applied the aloe lotion to Jenna's back. To Jenna's delight, they had shared a shower when they returned to the ship, but the hot water brought out the pain of the sunburn she did not realize she had received. Instead of it being a precursor to love making, it triggered the demand for anything that would sooth the pain.

"A little to the right . . . oooh . . . lower . . . oooh . . . down a little . . . is it red?"

"I'm afraid so," said Marcus as he continued the lotion application on the back of her legs. "The aloe should help relieve the pain but clothing will be a real issue."

"Well, I won't wear a bra and I have a fancy large loose sweat shirt I can wear. With a full long skirt, no one but you will know I am not wearing anything underneath," responded Jenna, a little smug.

Marcus had been aroused in the shower but now treating Jenna's sunburn and sensing her severe pain, that desire had totally disappeared but his mind did wander. *I wonder if Angelina got burned?* he thought. *Applying lotion to her back could be exciting.*

His thoughts were quickly interrupted as Jenna yelled, "Easy, my legs must have really got it."

"I'm sorry. Look, Jenna, we have to hurry. I will help you dress. We have to go to dinner with the group. We don't know if and when the cartel or the Mafia will contact Franco, but if it occurs, we want to be there if possible."

The Promenade Aruba was portrayed as a blend of fine yet casual European dining and it met all their expectations. It had both an inside dining area fashioned as an Italian villa complete with Tuscan columns and outside patio dining with light decorated trees separating the tables that were adorned with glass chimney candles. A square table for eight had been assembled for the Gambioni party. They were only seven but with Sal's assistant invited along, they rounded up to eight. Seating was not at all to Jenna's liking. It put her and Marcus facing the Gambionis and also put Angelina on the corner next to Marcus. He immediately took advantage of this and involved her in close conversation.

They were partway through the antipasto when Marcus spotted Alphonse being seated with a stranger at a table some distance away. Looking at Franco across the table, he said, "Franco, it looks like Alphonse has found a friend."

Turning around and spotting them, Franco said, "Oh yes, that's Luciano Guerra, an old friend of mine from Palermo."

All conversation around the table ceased and all eyes went to the table where Alphonse was sitting. Marcus noticed that the expression on Martina's face changed from relaxed to what appeared to be serious concern. She turned to Marcus and gave a quick nod and picked up her napkin and coughed. Marcus grabbed Jenna's hand next to him under the table and gave it a little squeeze. Sal broke the silence, turning to Franco, saying,

"Oh yes, Franco, you mentioned him to me on the drive back to the ship earlier."

———•—•———

It was almost nine o'clock when they all assembled in the captain's cabin: Jenna, Marcus, Martina, Security Officer Smith and the captain. The ship had left Aruba at seven, but Franco had insisted on treating all to cappuccino onboard since they had to leave the restaurant early to get back to the ship in time for sailing. It was only after enjoying the coffee, recapping the day and many thank you's that all excused themselves and went their separate ways.

As they sat down around the captain's conference table, Martina opened the conversation saying, "Well, there you have it!"

"There you have what?" asked Marcus.

"The Sicilian Mafia contact with Franco has occurred. I know that Luciano character from mug shots I've seen at the home office. There is no question, he is the contact."

"Well, that's one link in the chain, but we don't know if another drug cartel is involved and who they might be," said Marcus. Looking at Martina, he asked, "Do you think Franco will cave to the Sicilian family?"

"They can be very persuasive," said Martina. "Cartagena tomorrow could be very interesting," she continued.

"We are not there yet," said the captain. "We still have several hours at sea. Let's hope we don't have any issues on board during that time."

"I truly don't think we'll have a problem," said Security Officer Smith. "With the deportation of the accused assailant this morning and our review of all the remaining crewmembers we boarded in St. Thomas, I feel pretty confident we shouldn't have any issues during our sailing tonight."

"Let's hope so," responded the captain. Looking at Jenna and Marcus, he said,

"You certainly have your work cut out for you tomorrow." Then looking at Martina, he asked,

"Are you aware of any shore excursion packages the Gambionis are signed up for tomorrow?"

"Yes, and that's the interesting part," said Martina. "Adriana and Angelina are signed up to go on the morning tour of the Old City, followed by the shuttle run to the Pierino Gallo Plaza. The Shopping Host onboard recommended she visit the emerald shop in the Plaza that goes by her name. I believe the altercation we witnessed this morning between her and Franco resulted in her planning on an expensive shopping tour. What Franco's plans are, I don't know."

Jenna, now standing up and walking around the small office, said, "I'm sorry, this sunburn is really smarting." Looking at Marcus, she continued, "Sal mentioned last night that he and Franco were being met at the ship by someone but he wouldn't go into any further detail. From what we learned in St. Thomas, I would bet it's someone from the Londoño cartel."

"I have arranged to be part of the cruise staff on the shore excursions that Angelina and Adriana will be on so I have them covered," said Martina, and looking at Marcus and then Jenna, she continued, "How you cover Franco is beyond me. I am sure that in addition to whatever they have planned with the Londoño cartel, there will be some further, not necessarily wanted or expected, contact initiated by the Sicilian Mafia."

CHAPTER 7

Cartagena

The Golden Duchess slowed to six knots as it approached the Boca Chica channel entrance to the Cartagena harbor. The shell door on Deck Four was open and the pilot boat speeded alongside. Two men were standing on the pilot boat bow. Watching the wave motion of the pilot boat and the Golden Duchess, the first man jumped and was caught and helped aboard. Instead of pulling away, the pilot boat continued alongside with a call from its speaker saying, "Second pilot to come aboard," and almost simultaneously the second man on the bow of the pilot boat jumped toward the Golden Duchess and luckily was caught by two crewmen and pulled aboard. The officer in charge called the bridge and informed them two pilots had been boarded and would be brought up.

The senior pilot entered the bridge and Captain Hempsell greeted him as an old friend and said, "You brought a helper, I understand. Where is he?"

"He should be along shortly. He stopped in the head on the way up. He is new and I don't think he has his sea legs yet. He looked a little green on the trip out. Frankly, I was surprised this morning when they assigned him to me and told me to take him along. With both the cruise and container ship traffic increasing, they are trying to build up the pilot staff. He obviously is one of the new hires. He supposedly knows the waters here well as he was a local fisherman for several years. He should be up here shortly. The port is calm this morning; I should have you dockside in about 40 minutes."

———•••———

Jenna woke with a start. The door to the bathroom was open and she could hear the shower. Rolling over, she realized it was Marcus since he was not in bed. *How did I sleep with Marcus not waking me?* she thought. Then rolling back to get out of bed, she let out a small cry, "Oooh." The sunburn still smarted. Her mind began to spin. *Well, it wasn't the erotic night I hoped for, but Marcus did sleep with me. It had to have been several times during the night that I cried out and he applied the aloe where it was hurting.*

Before her thoughts could go further, Marcus said, "Oh good, you are awake," as he came out of the bathroom in one of the white terrycloth robes the Duchess provided in the mini suites. "We are coming into port and I would like to be first off. In fact, I'll call Security Officer Smith while you shower to see if he can arrange it like he did in St. Thomas."

"Thank you, Marcus. The aloe did help a lot. I'm sorry I kept you up. Why do you want to be first off? I thought we agreed that there was no way we could follow Franco, and Martina will be with the rest of the Gambionis on a tour. Marcus, you said we would just take the shuttle into town and do a little exploring on our own."

"I know I said that but I thought if we could be in the cruise center when he, and he will probably have Sal with him, are out there waiting to be picked up, we might be able to see who picks them up. Maybe get a description we can send back. Further, with that Sicilian Mafia guy we saw at dinner last night, we don't have any idea if there is going to be a Londoño connection or what.

Please, let's get going. When you finish showering, I'll lotion you up again before you dress."

———·—·———

There was a hard knock on Sal's door. "Coming," he called out. His assistant said, "I'll get it."

"No, let me," said Sal. Looking through the peep hole he was surprised to see Franco and opened the cabin door immediately.

"Mr. Gambioni, what's the matter?" Sal saw an expression of fear in Franco's face that he had never seen before. "Please come in. Sit down," he said. "Get some water," he called to his assistant.

Franco sat down. Sipping the water and speaking in almost a whisper, he said, "While walking on the deck, I was visited by someone I have never seen before, but he knew me by name and spoke in Sicilian Italian. He said he had been instructed to inform me that considering our health and well-being, it would be in the best interests of me and my family if I would have nothing further to do with the Londoño cartel and further, I will be contacted by the Calista cartel."

"Who was he? Did he give you a name?"

"No. That's all he said and then he left. I am sure this is the doings of the Sicilian Mafia. Luciano Guerra said this would happen. Sal, I am concerned about our meeting with Londoño and what could happen. I have never had any doings with the Sicilian Mafia in the past but I have heard they have their contacts in the states and can be very persuasive." "Mr. Gambioni, I will be with you and my assistant will also be watching. Señora Londoño assured Alphonse that we would be picked up at the ship. I'm sure that will happen. We don't know anything about this Calisto cartel. I would just proceed with what we originally planned."

———·—·———

The front of the cruise terminal appeared to be a huge circus of confused passengers, tour buses lined up with tour guides holding signs in front of each, and two long lines of cabs and unmarked cars queued up to pick up passengers. Add to that a bright sunny day and the ever-present humidity of the Caribbean. Unfortunately, the huge cruise ship portside blocked the ever-present breeze coming off the water.

Marcus and Jenna positioned themselves just outside the terminal in view of the taxi stand area. They were off to the side of the entrance. For them to be noticed, passengers would have to turn around and look back toward the ship. They were soon rewarded for their wait.

"Look, there are Sal and Franco coming out the door. It looks like they are heading to the taxi stand. No, they are just standing a little in front of the taxi lineup," said Jenna.

Just then a black limo pulled in front of the cabs, its windows tinted so no one could see inside. The driver rolled his window down and called, "Señor Gambioni, please come," and the side passenger door opened.

"This must be it," said Sal. "Get in, Mr. Gambioni. I'll go around and get in the other side."

Sal closed the door and took one step but was practically knocked down as the tires screeched and the car sped away. Marcus and Jenna ran down the steps, grabbed the staggering Sal and said in unison, "Are you OK?"

"Yes, but they got Franco."

"Who got Franco?" asked Marcus.

"I don't know, but I don't think that was the pickup we were waiting for."

"What do you mean?"

"Marcus, we were . . . . "

Before Sal could finish the sentence, another limo pulled up and through the rolled down window Sal recognized Ricardo, who called out to him, "Señor Indelicato, where is Señor Gambioni?"

"We have a problem," replied Sal.

"Get in, I can't hold up the queue," said Ricardo.

Sal called to Marcus and Jenna, "Later," and jumped into the back seat of the limo, which immediately drove off.

"Holy shit! We have trouble," said Marcus. Then, seeing Jenna pulling her cell phone out, he asked, "Who are you calling?"

"You are lucky, Marcus, that your partner has a photographic memory. I got the tags on both the limos. I'm calling Martina. She told me earlier that that she would be contacting her office while here. Evidently Interpol has an office here. During the Cartagena cleanup by the Colombian government, an Interpol office was established here as a part of the war on drugs. I'm sure she may be able to help."

Jenna had put Martina's cell phone number on speed dial and as she responded to Marcus, she put the phone to her ear. Martina answered on the first ring and Jenna said, "Martina. Where are you? We have a situation. Let me give you two license numbers while they are still clear in my mind."

After reciting the license numbers to Martina, Jenna explained what they had just witnessed, ending with, "Martina, is there anything we can do?"

"Look, I will contact the Interpol office and give them these plate numbers, turn my tour over to my assistant and meet you there. You guys catch a cab. I'll text you the address when we hang up."

The door slammed, the tires screeched, and Franco was pulled back into his seat, yelling, "Wait, wait, my *protezione del corpo*."

"You won't be needing him," came a gruff Spanish-accented voice from the front seat.

Because of the heavily tinted glass and the bright sun, it took a few minutes before Franco's eyes adjusted to the dim interior of the limo. It was then he became aware that someone was seated next to him and looking at him, he realized it was Luciano Guerra.

"What, what, how did you get here?" he said.

"Private plane from Aruba last night. After your ship left port," responded Luciano in Sicilian Italian.

"The driver does not understand Italian. He is taking us to a meeting with representatives of the Calista cartel. Relax, you are safe, I assure you. After our meeting, you will be safely taken back to the ship. Don't worry."

Somehow these words coming from a Sicilian he had just met the day before gave little comfort to Franco Gambioni.

"I am sorry," said Ricardo rolling down all the windows of the limo as they drove out of the cruise terminal area. "The air conditioner went out this morning when I picked up the car."

The breeze from the windows felt cool on Sal's perspiration-soaked shirt and collecting his thoughts, he explained to Ricardo what had happened and Ricardo responded with, "*Hija de puta, triple jue pute*," almost yelling the phrases.

Sal didn't understand a word he was saying, but assumed it was swearing and interrupted with, "Ricardo, where are we going? What can we do? I'm worried for Franco."

Then in almost a completely calm voice, Ricardo responded in broken English, "Señor Indelicato, we go airport. Pick up Señor Romano. He on morning Aruba plane. We go to Londoños."

The Interpol office was in the Old Town walled section of Cartagena on the second floor of the building whose address Martina had texted to them. From the outside it appeared as a normal two-story building with a large balcony. No one would guess that the building housed a large office area on the second floor. And there was no indication of its occupants posted outside. Inside was a small reception area with an armed guard posted. Upon identifying themselves, Marcus and Jenna were ushered into a special elevator that went directly to the second floor.

As the door opened, they were surprised to see Martina greeting them saying, "Welcome to Interpol South America. Come, follow me." Leading them through a small maze of cubicles occupied with agents busy on computers, Martina continued, "This is our central office for all South America. It is located here as a covert precaution. We will be in the operations room at the end of this maze."

"I'm impressed," said Marcus. "By the way, how did you get here so fast?"

"I was leading a tour of the Old Town that is just a few blocks from here, so after your call, I was here in a matter of minutes. We already have your limos under surveillance. You will see."

Entering the room, Marcus and Jenna were amazed: there, a whole wall of monitors were flashing and two monitors at eye level clearly displayed the limos parked in front of what appeared to be apartment buildings. Almost in unison, Jenna and Marcus uttered, "Wow."

Sensing their surprise, Martina introduced Agent Hernandez, who was seated at the small conference table in the middle of the room. "You are obviously surprised," said Agent Hernandez. "Let me explain. Let's just call this Cartagena 101."

"I don't understand," said Jenna.

"I will try to be brief," said Agent Hernandez. "It became critical for Colombia to clean up Cartagena. During the peak of the drug cartel crime sprees throughout the country, cruise ship companies were eliminating Cartagena from their itineraries. The Colombian government made a major effort to make Cartagena a safe port, which it is today. Now that it is, it attracts commercial investment. The high-rises you see throughout the city are most all residential properties financed as major investment opportunities. And, it is not at all unusual to see drug money being utilized to finance such endeavors."

"That's all very interesting, but what does it have to do with Franco Gambioni?" asked Marcus.

"As a part of maintaining security in the city, the government has installed considerable video street surveillance. If you look at the screens over there," Agent Hernadez pointed to the two screens depicting the limos, "you see the two limos in question parked in front of two high-rises. One is owned by the Londoño cartel (under another name, of course) and houses their business office in the penthouse on the 44th floor. The other is parked in front of a high-rise owned by the Calista cartel that has their operations office in the penthouse on the 33rd floor. That condo was built a year before the Londoño condo, and I'm sure they weren't happy to see the Londoño condo go up 11 floors higher."

"If you know all this and the local government as well, why don't they just go in and raid the places?" asked Marcus.

"Welcome to Colombia. The laws, how they are implemented, and where in the country is a complete puzzle. Even after the war on drugs, the cleanup by your government and Colombia and the demise of the Medellin cartel locally, there still exists an intertwining of social, political, government, and drug cartel influence. We, of course, have no power in this country but are allowed to have our offices here and coordinate with local authorities. Further, they do provide us access to their city monitoring system. Local authorities tell us that as long as no local crime is committed by the perceived drug cartel condo management, they won't be bothered."

"This is ridiculous," clamored Marcus." We know they are holding Franco and Sal."

"Do we?" said Agent Hernandez. "From your report you claimed they got into those limos voluntarily. How do you know they are being held by anybody? Look, our intelligence indicates that Pablo Londoño is reported to be in Cartagena and if that is true, he is probably in his condo suite. As long as his presence causes no local trouble, the local authorities will give him carte blanche. We have no Intel at this time about the Calisto cartel but we can be sure if they are endeavoring to cut some sort of deal with Franco, someone in authority is in their penthouse suite. The best we can do at this time is just sit tight and monitor Franco and Sal's whereabouts and see how the cartels work the issue. Remember, these small cartels that exist today have a somewhat love-hate relationship with each other as they coexist endeavoring to equitably divide up the market place."

"Look!" called Jenna, pointing at one of the video monitors. "Isn't that Franco coming out of the condo building? It appears he is getting into the limo."

"Not to worry," said Agent Hernadez. "We have people on the ground; he will be followed."

The doors to the elevator opened and the lovely though treacherous Señora Londoño held out her hand to Sal and Alphonse, saying, "Greetings, Señor Indelicato, Señor Romano, welcome to Cartagena, and where is Señor Gambioni?" Behind Señora Londoño was a huge living area, lavishly furnished and at the far end were sliding glass doors that appeared to go out to a deck overlooking the city and harbor.

As she led them in the direction of the deck, Alphonse said, "Apologies, Señora, I have just heard from him by cell phone and he assures me he will be here shortly. Please let me explain what happened. No, better Sal, you explain."

Two large picture windows on the right hand wall overlooked the beach while the wall to the left, decorated with modern art, accommodated two sliding doors that apparently led to the remaining rooms of the penthouse. "*Por favor*," replied Señora opening the sliding doors to the patio, "I am sure Pablo would be interested as well."

Being the tallest building in the area, walking on the deck gave one the feeling of walking on a cloud floating over the city. A rather large, very tanned gentleman sat at a small cocktail table surrounded by four potted palms. Setting his drink down and getting up as they approached, eyes flashing, addressing the señora in a loud voice, he said in Spanish, "Who are these people? Where is Señor Gambioni?"

———•·•———

All conversation came to a halt. The four sat at the conference table in the Interpol operations room staring at the monitors as if they were watching a movie and they were waiting for something major to happen. It was so quiet Marcus thought he could hear his heart beating, and the air rushing in and out as he breathed through his mouth sounded like a wind tunnel. Finally breaking the silence, he said, "Martina, can we get a secure line to CIA offices in New York?"

"Yes, no problem. Come with me."

"Jenna, stay with Agent Hernandez and keep an eye on the limos. See if Franco goes to the Londoños next. I'll give the home office our status and find out if we have any further orders."

With that, Martina and Marcus left the operations room. Alone with a comely young American, Agent Hernandez jumped at the opportunity to know her better.

"Agent Adams, how long have you been with the CIA?" he asked.

"It's been a little over two years. Marcus and I were recruited in our senior year at New York University. Quite frankly, it's been pretty boring and not at all what we expected. Until we were sent on this undercover assignment, we were doing background investigations. It was really surprising that we got this assignment. The FBI handles all the Mafia activity in New York. I guess because this was happening outside the US, they felt obligated to ask the CIA to help with this. I think we were selected because we were young enough to pass as newlyweds. At least that's what our boss told us. It beats doing the paperwork job we were doing, and hey, a cruise vacation at government expense, not bad."

"The limo that picked up Franco outside the Calisto building just pulled up at the Londoño complex," interrupted Agent Hernandez, who was watching the monitors as he chatted with Jenna.

"I am sure Marcus is reporting to our boss that Franco is dealing with either or both of the Calisto and Londoño cartels. That's really all we were supposed to find out and report about."

"Well, it might not be that simple," responded Agent Hernandez. "If the Sicilian Mafia are connected and more than one cartel is involved, the routing of drug shipments could get complicated. This would have a severe impact on the FBI's effort to mitigate drug traffic coming into the US. I am sure any information concerning this possibility is critical to their operation."

"I hadn't thought about that," said Jenna.

"Interpol has been concerned with the possible expansion of the Sicilian Mafia. The Mafia's involvement with this potential new Gambioni drug operation is of primary interest to them," continued Agent Hernandez.

Suddenly the door burst open and Marcus, followed by Martina, rushed in shouting, "Jenna, we have an issue and it could become serious."

"Marcus, what's up? You look upset."

"Luigi Santori was found shot to death in Brooklyn this morning, execution style. He was Franco's underboss. Franco might not know this yet. The police and FBI don't know whether this was a rival family or something else. In any case, we are assigned to continue to watch the Gambionis."

"Whoa! They could be in danger. Do we tell Sal?" asked Jenna.

"I don't think we have to. I am sure he will know soon enough.

But we can certainly comment to him about it as according to headquarters, it was in the Daily News this morning. Knowing about it wouldn't be out of character for us at all."

"This could be the Sicilian Mafia firing a warning shot at Franco, endeavoring to convince him that he should follow their desires as to which cartel to do business with," said Martina. "They have been known to be able to contract murder in other countries with little regard for consequences."

"Also, as I said earlier, there is a love-hate relationship among the cartels here," said Agent Hernandez, "and opportunities for the rich US market are certainly coveted by all. The Calisto cartel, finding out that the Londoño cartel has a potential deal going on with Franco, could also spark deadly action between the two. Oh, nothing will happen here in Cartagena, but elsewhere in Colombia or whereever, watch out."

"By the way," Marcus said, looking at Jenna, "we have also been told to maintain our cover. So letting Sal know who we are is out of the question. We are facing five days before we get back to New York, with a stop at San Juan. It could be a perilous journey."

"Do you think Franco is in danger?" asked Jenna.

"No, not at all," said Agent Hernandez. "He is the prize: a doorway to a new drug market in the US. However, anyone around or associated with him is open game if it helps get the market in the desired camp."

Despite all the tension in the situation being discussed, Marcus could see the lust in Agent Hernandez's eyes as he spoke and looked at Jenna and it bothered him. This was new to him; he had never really felt this emotion before. To shake it, he quickly turned his view to the monitors and spotted activity. "They are coming out of the Londoño building. It looks like Sal and Franco are getting in one limo and Alphonse in the other. He is probably off to the airport and Sal and Franco are going back to the ship."

"We have accomplished all we can here," said Martina. "I will try to catch up with my tour. You and Jenna might want to come along. The last stop is the Palace of the Inquisition, also known as the torture museum. There should be enough room on the bus so you can get back to the ship with the tour."

———————

"Would Mr. Franco Gambioni and Mr. Salvatore Indelicato please contact the passenger services desk," blared the ship's PA system.

"You know what that means," said Jenna, looking down at the dock from their balcony. The tour buses had all departed and there were no cabs parked in front of the cruise terminal. The crew was busy dismantling the comfort station at the main gangway.

"What?" asked Marcus.

"It means they have no record of them returning to the ship. When they start calling names just before sailing, it is a clear indication that passengers have not returned from shore. They have a record of them leaving but not of returning. It's the captain's call how long he will wait and they probably are contacting the ship's agent on shore to see if any contact has been made there."

"I bet Adriana and Angelina are in a panic," said Marcus.

"I'm sure. They both seemed a little uneasy on the tour when we joined it with Martina. I spoke to Angelina and she commented that her father told her he had business and would see them back on board."

"Oh, look. That's the Londoño cruiser coming across the bay. I'm sure," said Marcus, pointing toward the large yacht approaching the dock just forward of the Golden Duchess. The fishtail plumes rising up from its sides gave an indication it was going at top speed.

"Well, I hope they radioed the bridge. They have already

stowed all boarding ramps but one and are beginning to man the mooring lines. We are obviously preparing to sail."

———•·•———

As Marcus slowly applied the aloe lotion to Jenna, she commented, "Oh, that feels so good. A little lower, over to the right. Oh."

After the hot humid day in Cartagena, she felt a shower was definitely in order and as soon as the Golden Duchess left the dock, she was back in the cabin. While she showered, Marcus stayed out on the balcony watching the boat traffic as the ship moved slowly through the Boca Chica channel. The pilot boat followed a short distance behind the ship, anticipating a pickup when they reached the open sea.

Marcus had left the door open to the balcony when he came in answering Jenna's call from her bed, where she lay on a towel in the altogether. Continuing to lightly rub the lotion, he became aroused and thought *She does have a beautiful body. How did I not notice her before.*

The scene was quickly shattered as loud voices came from the balcony below. "*Che cavolo*, Franco, you promised no business. *Porca miseria*, you almost missed the ship!" screamed Adriana. "*Testa di cazzo*, I saw you and Sal board. You are lucky the captain waited. What took you so long to come back to our cabin?"

"Please, Adriana, calm down. People can hear you. We had a crisis back home."

"What?"

"Luigi was killed last night. You are lucky I am here. I almost went home with Alphonse."

"Oh, my God, do they know who did it? Who will take charge?" As their voices quieted down, Marcus left Jenna and went out to the balcony so see if he could hear more. Franco answered Adriana but in a very low voice.

"Giordano, Luigi's number two is in charge. I just spoke to

him on my cell. When Alphonse arrives, they will get back to me with any new information. We will be at sea so it will have to be by email. Let's hope the satellite that the ship talks to is working properly."

With those last few words, Marcus heard the sliding door slam shut and all went quiet, indicating that Franco and Adriana had gone inside. To be sure, he went over to the balcony rail. The balcony below was empty; the pilot boat had caught up with the ship and was approaching the open shell door on Deck Four. The pilot transfer occurred and the ship began to increase speed.

———•—•———

Vines, the wine, sushi and tapas bar in the Atrium, was totally vacated except for Sal and Angelina. They were seated at a table tucked in the back next to a window and behind the tasting bar. Someone walking around the Piazza would never see them.

"Thanks for meeting me, Sal. I really can't handle it when my father and mother get into a shouting match. This time it was loud and outside on the balcony. My mother was swearing. I just had to get out of there."

"I understand. But you should know your Dad is under a lot of pressure right now."

"Oh, because you were late getting back to the ship," said Angelina with a little smile on her face.

"No, it's far more complicated than that," said Sal in a serious tone, giving her a sobering look.

"Your father tries to keep you unaware of what he does for your safety, and I normally would agree with that philosophy. However, contrary to his desires and because my assistant and I are responsible for your well being as well as his and your mother's, I believe you should be aware of the current situation. I can't get into details, but your father just received word that the person he left in charge of his business was found dead in Brooklyn last night."

Color drained from Angelina's face and her hands started

to quiver. Sal reached across the table, grabbing them both as he continued, "There are two competing organizations here in Colombia that want to do business with him and their methods of convincing him are not particularly savory."

Sal could see the fear in her eyes as he spoke and he wrestled with his own emotions. He felt she should be aware, but his feelings for her were in flux seeing her so upset. "This is further complicated by pressure being exerted from a family in Sicily whose member you met at dinner the other night in Aruba. They also are known for committing unsavory acts to accomplish their desires."

Tears began to form in Angelina's eyes. Her mouth had begun to quiver and color had completely drained from her face. Sal squeezed her hands and tried to speak in a soothing tone, "Though it's prudent to be cautious, I believe there should be no apparent danger facing you or your family during the rest of the cruise. We only have one more port, San Juan, which is American. Remember, I will always be near. It's my job."

Neither was conscious of when it occurred, but they were standing, wrapped in each other's arms, Angelina's head resting on Sal's shoulder. Both were totally unaware of Adriana approaching.

CHAPTER 8

Tumultuous Waters

The Peterson cabin was dark as night. Marcus had not opened the balcony drape when he left for exercise. Jenna woke with a jolt as the cabin phone rang. Rolling over, she realized that Marcus was not in bed. She fumbled for the phone, which was on his side of the bed.

"Hello, Jenna Peterson here." *I could get used to that name,* she thought.

"Myla here, good morning."

"Oh, good morning Myla, how are you? Did you manage to get on shore yesterday?"

"I am afraid not. Captain Hempsell kept me busy."

"Oh, sorry about that. It really is a great port. What can I do for you?"

"The captain would like to reconvene our security meeting. He would be pleased if you and Marcus could join him and the others in his cabin at 8:00. Martina and Security Officer Smith will be there. He wants to have a recap of what took place yesterday on shore."

"Well, I believe Marcus is up at the fitness center, but he should be back soon. When he doesn't see me at the Windows Court, I am sure he will either call or come back to the cabin. It's only 7:00 now, so I'm sure we can be there. Later, Myla," Jenna finished and hung up the phone. Rolling back to her side and staring up at the ceiling, her mind began to spin. *Are we in the start of a relationship or not? These last two nights my sunburn sort of canceled all thoughts of passion. Marcus does seem attentive, but is there an emotional connection? Yesterday was all business in Cartagena. I felt that first night of passion ignited something but now I really don't know. Was I wrong to seduce him? What do I need to be doing differently to find out?*

Her thoughts were shattered as Marcus burst through the cabin door, turning on the lights and calling, "Jenna? Are you alright? You weren't at the Windows Court."

"I'm sorry, Marcus, I overslept. The sunburn pain finally subsided." Looking at the clock on the bedstand, Jenna continued, "I better get up right now."

Marcus opened the drapes to the balcony, letting the bright sun light up the cabin. He looked relieved but a little surprised as Jenna popped out of bed and headed for the bathroom. "Oh!" she called back, "Myla called and we are due in the Captain's cabin in 50 minutes."

———•—•———

Marcus and Jenna had no sooner left Captain Hempsell's cabin when over the PA system came, "This is the bridge speaking. In ten minutes time we will commence a crew exercise. Passenger areas will not be affected. At the sounding of the ship's horn, all assigned crew will report to their duty stations."

Grabbing Jenna's hand and moving into a fast walk, Marcus said, "Quick, Jenna, we have to get aft up on the Sun Deck. The captain said that we would have the best view of the planned exercise there."

As they raced aft along the Lido Deck, Jenna asked, "Marcus, were you as surprised as I was that he said they had a major crew change in Cartagena? Why Cartagena? You would think they would wait until San Juan."

"I asked him that while you and Martina were talking, and he said that was true in the past but due to the new US immigration procedures, most ships are doing all crew changes outside of the US. Further, based on the issues we faced out of St. Thomas, Security Officer Smith told me he and Martina would be going over the new crew member lists to see if any names pop out as possible troublemakers. Evidently there were several Italians and Central Americans on the list."

Racing up the stairs to the Sun Deck, they reached the aft rail and Marcus, gazing out at the sea behind the ship, spotted something and shouted, "Holy shit, I know we are not on the eastern coast of Africa, but Jenna, look. That open boat powered by two large outboard motors sure as hell resembles a Somali skiff. It's exactly like the ones we saw in our briefings on Somali pirates and it's moving up fast."

"This is either a very realistic training exercise or we have a problem," said Jenna.

———•—•———

Sal sat with Franco at the laptop he had brought along and looked on as Franco tried to email Alphonse back in Brooklyn. "Sal, it's formal night tonight and Angelina and Adriana are at the hairdressers. I would like to have some sort of dialog with Alphonse before they get back. I may have to fly back to New York from San Juan."

"That will go over like a lead balloon with Adriana," said Sal.

In a somewhat irritated voice Franco said, "Sal, I pay you to protect my family, not give me marital advice."

"Sorry, Mr. Gambioni," said Sal as he visualized the tirade Adriana would have if Franco told her he was going home and leaving her and Angelina on board to finish the cruise.

Just then an email popped up on the computer screen. "It's slow but at least we are communicating," said Franco, clicking the email to open it.

"Oh shit!" they said in unison.

———— • ————

In addition to being formal night on the ship, it was Italian night in the Portofino Dining Room. The serving staff were all dressed in red and white striped shirts as Venetian gondoliers. Red, white and green streamers were strung between the chandeliers and Italian music was playing softly in the background, all creating a festive ambience in the dining room. Franco insisted on having the Petersons join the Gambioni table and went as far as sending a formal invitation to Marcus and Jenna that was in their cabin mailbox when they returned from witnessing the crew exercise.

The Gambionis and Sal were already seated when Jenna and Marcus arrived, and they were totally surprised to see Franco stand up as they approached, saying, "Welcome to our newlywed honeymooners."

Marcus, completely taken aback and thinking, *what is happening here, this is surely not the stoic Franco we know,* extended his hand, saying, "Thank you Mr. Gambioni." He then helped Jenna to her seat.

Franco sat down and, motioning to the waiter to pour the wine, continued, "Please, enjoy our favorite Nebbiolo from the Piedmont region of Italy."

Jenna, slipping her hand over to Marcus under the table, gave him a questioning look, thinking, *What is going on here? This is not the Franco Gambioni we know.*

As all glasses were filled, Franco raised his in a toast and said, "To our captain and crew, who saved us from the Somali pirates."

Raising his glass with the others, Marcus said, "Hear, hear." And all sipped. Marcus continued, saying, "But there were no Somali pirates. It was just a training exercise. This ship is scheduled to go to the Middle East at the completion of this cruise, and this exercise was just part of their preparation for sailing in that region."

"But I saw them firing at the ship until they were knocked out of their boat by the high-pressure water spray from our crew, and then we speeded up and outran them," said Franco.

"They were firing blanks; it was all staged as part of the exercise. This was our day to visit the bridge and the captain explained it to us. The skiff and the pirates are cruise company employees stationed in Cartagena. We really didn't outrun them. What you didn't see or know was, we also simulated directing a high frequency sound wave at them, which would be extremely painful to their ears. This is the current defense being used against pirates."

"Well, so be it," said Franco. "*Evviva gli sposi!*"

"Thank you again," said Jenna.

"Oh, you know Italian," said Franco, with a questioning look at Jenna.

"Not really. I have just attended some Italian weddings."

Conversation continued throughout the dinner on a casual note, focusing on Italian cuisine and Italian traditions. Jenna sensed the dynamics of the table had definitely changed. Rather than Angelina, Marcus seemed to be paying more attention to her and Sal appeared to be totally attracted to Angelina. Observing facial expressions and comments, she also became conscious of Adriana's displeasure at the apparent blossoming relationship between Angelina and Sal.

This was also noted by Marcus. His thoughts, *Sal, you appear to be breaking your rule and Mamma Gambioni doesn't seem to approve.*

His thoughts were broken when Franco got up and said, "Sal, take Angelina dancing with the Petersons. Adriana and I will retire. We have a busy day planned in San Juan tomorrow."

It was almost a command, which appeared to please Sal and

Angelina, but not Adriana. Before she could say anything, Franco grabbed her hand, escorting her out of the dining room.

Sal immediately addressed the Petersons, saying, "I am not sure you guys were planning on going dancing. I'm sorry, my boss can get a little demanding at times."

Jenna grabbed Marcus's hand and squeezed, saying to Sal, "No problem. We would love to go dancing with you. It's off to the Voyagers Lounge. By the way, your boss appears to be in a much better temperament than usual. What's going on in San Juan tomorrow?"

"It's a little complicated," responded Sal. "Let's go."

Adriana continued to chip at Franco as they made their way back to their cabin, and he continued to ignore her. Their cabin door had no sooner closed when Franco turned to his wife and, speaking in a firm tone he hadn't used all evening, said, "Adriana, I try to protect you and we both try to shield Angelina from our business. What I tell you now should go nowhere."

Adriana sat down. The tone in her husband's voice was a clear message to be quiet, listen, and don't comment. Franco continued, "There has been a massive FBI raid in Manhattan; all four of the other families were affected. The charges are expected to range from gambling to racketeering and murder. Alphonse is quite sure no one in our family has been arrested. Why, it is not clear. The murder of Luigi is being completely overlooked by the local authorities. Again, why is not clear. Alphonse attended a meeting of the commission and all of the other families swore they were not responsible for Luigi's death."

By now color had drained from Adriana's face and a clear expression of fear was evident as Franco spoke, "I had planned to fly back to NY from San Juan and let you and Angelina finish the cruise with Sal and his assistant, but that now appears to be a bad idea. Alphonse will keep me advised as we sail back to NY.

Our informers have indicated that so far there appear to be no charges pending for me or anyone in our organization."

An expression of relief began to appear on Adriana's face and without pause, Franco went on, "However, they further reported to Alphonse that they thought our activities on this cruise were being watched and reported to the FBI, but there was no indication by who or what organization. Adriana, I want you and Angelina to take advantage of any shore excursions in San Juan. Sal's assistant will be with you wherever you go. Maybe you could hook up with the Petersons. Sal and I are sure we will be contacted by those we met with in Cartagena, so we will not be with you."

Franco's pause allowed for Adriana's response, which she knew would be superficial but as a wife she had to say it. "Franco, please be careful."

The PA system chimed, followed by, "This is the Bridge. This is the Bridge. Will the medical response team report to Deck Five International Café. This is the Bridge, will the medical response team report to Deck Five, International Café."

Marcus rolled over. Looking at the clock, then shaking Jenna, he said, "Jenna, Jenna, did you hear that. Someone must be seriously hurt down in the piazza area."

"Marcus, I was sound asleep. What's the matter? What time is it?"

"It's 6:30. There appears to be a medical issue onboard. I believe that . . ."

Before Marcus could finish his sentence, came, "This is the Bridge. This is the Bridge. Will the medical trauma team report to Deck Five International Café. Will the medical trauma team report to Deck Five International Café."

"Marcus, this could be something serious. We should get up and get dressed," said Jenna.

"I agree," answered Marcus as he leaped from the bed and ran toward the bathroom.

———•—•———

Chime. "Good morning, ladies and gentlemen. This is the captain speaking. I apologize for disturbing you, but we have a medical evacuation team enroute and they should be here in ten minutes time. We will be evacuating the aft areas on deck 17 and 16 and all aft cabins on deck 15, 12, 11, and 10. We apologize for the inconvenience but please follow the instructions of the staff members."

"Gosh!" said Marcus as he opened the door to the balcony. "The ship is really slowing down and I can hear the chopper in the distance. Jenna, come out here. It's coming in. I can see it now."

Batabatabatabatabata. The sound of the chopper increased as it closed in on the ship.

"I wish we were up on the Lawn Court above Deck 17. I bet that's where it's setting down," continued Marcus. "They probably wouldn't let us near there if we were up there."

"I wonder who is being evacuated and why," said Jenna.

From their balcony Marcus and Jenna could see the helicopter coming in, but it was not visible as it hovered over the aft deck of the ship. "Look, Jenna, down on the promenade deck. It looks like a fire response team. I suspect all the precautions are in case the chopper hit something on the ship coming in and caused a crash," said Marcus.

"I hadn't thought about that," said Jenna, "but I guess it could happen."

After what seemed like a very short time, *Batbatbatabatabata.* The chopper came back into view and flew off in the direction of San Juan.

"That sure was a rapid transfer of whoever was being evacuated," said Marcus and as they came in from their balcony, the chimes from the PA sounded again, followed by, "*This is the captain speaking. The evacuation has been completed. At the current speed of the air rescue helicopter, the patient should be at the hospital in 25 minutes time. We wish her well. I thank you for your cooperation. All evacuated passengers may return to their cabins.*"

Almost immediately, the cabin phone rang and Marcus, answering it, said, "Marcus Peterson here."

"You're kidding!"

"Yes, certainly, right away."

Hanging up and turning to Jenna, he said, "That was Security Officer Smith. He would like to meet with us in the captain's cabin now. It was Martina who was evacuated."

————————

Seated around the captain's coffee table with Jenna and Marcus, Security Officer Smith related, "She was found unconscious in the staff entrance to the coffee bar in the International Café. Her vital signs appeared fine but the medical team couldn't bring her around. She appeared to have a head wound either from being hit or falling on the marble floor. She is being taken to acute care at Metropolitan Hospital in San Juan. The captain should be here shortly from the bridge."

"Is there any video in that area of the deck?" asked Marcus.

"Marcus!" interrupted Jenna, "We should be concerned about Martina's well being."

"Look, Jenna, she is obviously in good hands. We have a possible issue here that could affect the Gambionis and . . . ."

Before Marcus could finish, Captain Hempsell arrived, saying, "I assume you both have been briefed. I have just spoken to the hospital in San Juan. Martina is conscious but in pain and hasn't been able to respond as to what happened. I believe this is normal with a mild concussion. They believe she should be able to rejoin the ship when we arrive in San Juan."

"To respond to your earlier question, Marcus, there is no

video coverage in the part of the ship where she was found," said Security Officer Smith.

"Hopefully, Martina will be able to tell us what happened. However, if she was attacked from behind, she may not have a clue as to who attacked her," said the captain. "I believe we have a serious issue here. I also believe resolution will depend on what we learn from Martina. We will be arriving in San Juan within a couple of hours. Officer Smith, I suggest you query anyone who was in the area where Martina was discovered. Marcus, Jenna, entering San Juan Bay and docking at Old San Juan is quite picturesque. You are welcome to join me on the bridge and I will be able to point out some of the highlights as the pilot brings us in."

Looking at the ship's clock on the wall of his cabin, he continued, "We should be picking the pilot up about a half mile out from the bay and that should be in about one hour's time. The ship will slow to seven knots. Please come up. I will inform the officers on duty that you will be arriving." With that said, they all left his cabin and went separate ways.

CHAPTER 9

San Juan

Just a few miles out, the ship started to slow and the buildings of San Juan loomed into view. "Marcus, Jenna, look forward slightly to port," said Captain Hempsell. "See the pilot boat coming out?" Handing a set of binoculars to Marcus, he continued, "You should be able to see what's called the Fairway Buoy. It's red and is the first buoy of a long string of buoys we will be following in. The pilot boat will try to get into position to have the pilot transfer occur about when we reach that buoy. Once on board, he will be directing the helmsman the rest of the way in."

Marcus passed the binoculars to Jenna and asked, "Is that a fort on the port side of the entrance?"

"Yes, I'm not a historian but they say it dates back to the 1500s," said Captain Hempsell.

"Once we get into the bay we will be making a hard port turn and proceed directly into the cruise ship terminal. It is located within walking distance of Old San Juan. Actually, behind the fort you are looking at now."

"Captain, who is going to pick up Martina when we arrive?" asked Jenna.

"As a matter of fact, the ship's doctor and Deputy Captain Wardlow. Would you like to go along?" asked the captain.

"Yes, please," responded Jenna. Looking at Marcus, she

continued, "I know our orders were to report to the FBI office in San Juan and debrief them on our findings but considering what's happened, I think it best I follow up on Martina while you go to the FBI. I can call you with whatever I learn. I assume, since we are in US territory, they will have people assigned to follow the Gambionis and Sal while we are in port."

"Yes, the home office made that very clear when I spoke to them from Cartagena. We work together, but inside/outside the US, responsibility is clear and we don't violate that. Good plan, Jenna," said Marcus. Then turning to Captain Hempsell, he asked, "When do we sail?"

"Since we lost time with our 'Somali Pirate exercise' and won't be docking until afternoon, the home office has directed us to stay through the evening and not set sail for New York till midnight. Passengers will be directed to be onboard by 11:00 pm. The passengers will be happy about this, as Old San Juan comes alive after dark. Between the restaurants and nightclubs, the seven-square-block area becomes a party city, also a pickpocket haven, so watch yourself if you're out there tonight."

———————

The noise from the pilot boat engines was so loud it was impossible to hold a conversation. Martina sat in the forward cabin, her head filled with random thoughts: *The moment we got into that cab I just knew we were going to miss the ship. When I left Italy, I could never have imagined I would be here on a speed boat trying to catch up with a cruise ship.* Looking at Jenna sitting across the cabin from her, and Marcus standing on the aft deck where they would be jumping from, she thought, *They look so calm, I wonder if they are as scared as I am. They said it would be a piece of cake jumping aboard as the seas were so calm. Let's hope so. Marcus looks kind of cute out there. Sort of a James Bond manner about him. I'm sure glad they are not married. Maybe he could be my ticket to the US.*

Martina's obvious interest in Marcus did not go unnoticed by Jenna. *First I had Angelina. Now do I have to concern myself with Martina?* she asked herself.

"Prepare for boarding," came over the PA system on the pilot boat. Martina looked forward and seeing the ship and the opening at its side that they were approaching, her mind started spinning through the instructions they had been given. *We are to leap aboard the ship one at a time and the crew will be there to catch us. This will happen before the pilot leaps from the ship to the pilot boat. Jenna is to go first, then me, and then Marcus.*

One of the pilot boat crew helped her and Jenna out to the aft deck where Marcus was standing. Holding onto the rail, they watched as the boat came up alongside the ship. As the pilot boat got close, the aft deck of the pilot boat and the deck of the ship were almost at the same level, depending on the sea's swells. The crewman shouted, "Watch the swells. When we are parallel, leap. The crew will catch you. Who is first?"

Jenna got in position and at the instructed time just stepped aboard the ship, the crew catching her. It appeared that easy. *This shouldn't be that hard,* thought Martina as she got into position, but seeing the periodic space between the decks as the pilot boat rose and fell with the swells, she froze.

Jenna called from the ship, "It's easy, Martina. Don't worry, they will catch you."

Then the crewman yelled, "Now," and Martina leaped and was caught by one of the ship's crew.

"See, I told you it was easy," said Jenna to Martina as she landed and they both turned to watch Marcus.

Marcus positioned himself, watched the swells, and leaped. At that moment a swell caused the pilot boat to drop well below the ship's deck and separate away from the ship's side. Marcus fell to the sea.

"Marcus, no!" screamed Martina.

"Martina, Martina," said Jenna as she shook Martina, who was fully clothed, lying on the hospital bed.

"Oh, Oh, what, where am I?" said Martina and then shaking her head, she continued, "I must have fallen asleep while I was waiting for you guys. I'm sorry. What a nightmare I had. You wouldn't believe." Then looking at all who were in the room, she continued, "My, what a greeting party."

"How do you feel?" asked the ship's doctor. "They diagnosed you with a mild concussion but will release you to us if you feel well enough to come back aboard."

"My head's a little sore but I'm ready to go back to the ship. The food here sucks."

A serious expression engulfed Martina's face when she spotted Deputy Captain Wardlow and she continued, "Captain, we have an issue. I was on my way down to the International Café to meet with the other shore excursion leaders. I spotted a kitchen staff member who resembled another Mafia mug shot I had seen. He saw me coming toward him and forcibly pushed past me, knocking me down. That's the last I remember till I woke up here in the hospital. Then lightening her expression with a smile, she said, "They told me how I got here. It sounds like it was an exciting trip. I sort of wish I had been conscious to experience it."

"Let me assure you, there are better ways to ride in a helicopter," responded Deputy Captain Wardlow.

———•—•———

Sal had spotted the Londoño yacht in the marina next to the cruise ship terminal when they docked, so he was not surprised to see Ricardo outside the terminal building waving him and Franco to a limo parked in front of the cab line. He was not at all aware of the attractive young girl also standing outside the terminal in business clothes watching them. She had a cell phone up to her ear and had they been closer, he might have heard her say, "They are being waved to that forward black van in the cab line. Follow it."

———•———

Marcus was surprised to be immediately escorted to a briefing room when he identified himself at the reception desk in the FBI office. Three agents sat at the table facing him and after introductions, the one who appeared to be in charge said in an authoritative voice, "Tell us all you can about the Gambionis. Who they met. Where they went. Everything you can remember. And I believe you have a teammate. Where is she?" Without waiting for the answer, he continued, "We will arrange for a secure phone line so you can report to your office in New York when we finish here."

After having experienced the low-key, rather casual discussions he had with the Interpol agents in Cartagena, Marcus was a little put off by what was appearing to be a formal Q & A with the FBI agents. Straightening up in his chair, he said, "Thank you, sir. My teammate, Jenna Adams, should be calling me shortly. We had an issue on board before we arrived in San Juan and she is following up with it."

Removing a folded-up collection of papers from his jacket pocket and passing it across to the senior officer, Marcus continued, "I have prepared a chronological accounting of our activities and observations during the cruise and will go over the highlights if you wish. There has been an Interpol agent working with us and she suffered a debilitating encounter with someone on board early this morning and was evacuated to your local hospital. Jenna is there now and will call me when she gets more information."

"Yes, we were informed of Interpol's involvement. Please . . . ."

Before the senior FBI officer could finish, Marcus's cell phone rang and he answered, saying, "Yes, Jenna . . . . Really . . . . No, stay with Martina. I will include it with my report and tell the home office."

Closing his phone and looking across the table, Marcus said, "It appears we may have a Mafia family member from Sicily on board."

The soft sounds of jazz pianist Carli Munoz's were a welcome change for Jenna and Marcus, walking into Carlis Fine Bistro & Piano.

"Thank God we found this place," said Jenna. "True to Captain Hempsell's description, Old San Juan is a zoo at night. The crowds, musicians, people dancing in the streets is unbelievable."

"Yes, but earlier, when we walked past the fountain on Paseo de la Princesa and the sculpture garden, which was quiet and a little deserted, I had an eerie feeling from the way it was lit up. You sort of wanted to hurry along the cobblestones to get to where the action was," responded Marcus. Sitting at a table off in the corner, Jenna continued, "Do you think it was alright to go off the ship and leave Martina?"

"Look, Jenna, between the ship's doctor and Security Officer Smith, she is in good hands and the local FBI are supposedly watching the Gambionis. This evening is for us. Let's just enjoy!"

"By the way, Marcus, you may have a secret admirer and I don't mean me."

"What do you mean?"

"Well, on the way back from the hospital Martina told me she thinks you are cute and asked me if there was anything between us as she would like to get to know you better."

"What did you tell her?"

"I'm afraid I got a little huffy and screamed at her, 'Don't even think about it!'"

This brought a huge smile to Marcus's face and a little chuckle.

It was about 10:00 when Jenna and Marcus started back to the ship. Within a few blocks of the cruise terminal, the Golden Duchess became visible. With all her lighting, she was a beautiful sight.

"Isn't that fantastic?" said Jenna, pointing in the direction of the ship. Before Marcus could respond what sounded like a loud moan emanated from an alley they were passing.

Stopping Jenna and walking toward the ally, Marcus said, "Jenna, it sounds as if someone is hurt."

As they turned toward the alley, they were startled by a lone form that staggered out toward them and said, "Marcus, is that you?" and then collapsed on the ground.

Recognizing the voice, they ran to the body and helped him up, saying almost together, "Sal, Sal, what happened? Are you alright?"

"One of them hit me in the back of my head. It must have knocked me out." Then looking around, he continued, "Oh, shit. They must have taken Angelina."

"Who?" asked Marcus.

"I, I don't know. I am not sure."

"Calm yourself, Sal. Who? How many? When?"

"It had to have been here. We were walking up from the ship. I don't know how long I was out, but we left the ship at about 8:30, quarter to 9. I got back to the ship from a business meeting with Franco and he told me to take Angelina off to see Old San Juan before we sailed. I think he wanted some time private with Adriana."

"How many? Did you recognize any of them?"

Sal's face all of sudden lit up and he said, "Yes, yes, one of them was one of the bodyguards I saw in Cartagena when I visited the Calisto headquarters with Franco."

Maintaining cover, Marcus responded, asking, "Who is Calisto?"

Jenna had stepped away and was on her cell to the local FBI headquarters.

Angelina opened her eyes and slowly came to consciousness. *Ooh, what a headache,* she thought, and then sensing her position, *I'm being carried fireman style on somebody's back . . . That cloth someone put over my face from behind must have been chloroform or something like it. Geez, I went right out.*

"Juan, slow up. I think she is coming around," yelled the assailant carrying Angelina.

You bastards, thought Angelina as her mind came to full consciousness and began to spin. *You don't know who you did this to. Well, you are about to find out. I may appear to be a sweet helpless attractive young girl, but being brought up in Manhattan, I was street smart before I could walk, and while in college, I excelled in ballet and martial arts. You're about to find out what that means.*

"Ooh," she cried out as she began to struggle. As her assailant set her down, her feet no sooner had hit the ground than her fist shot straight to his Adam's apple, crushing his tracheae. Letting her go, he grabbed his neck and tried to get his breath but quickly fell to the ground, suffocating from lack of air. Not realizing what happened in the dark alley, the other assailant turned and, seeing his partner falling to the ground, and Angelina just standing there, rushed back. Concentrating on helping his partner, he was not at all expecting the karate blows he received from Angelina as he approached. Especially the last blow, which went to his neck.

With her assailants incapacitated on the ground, Angelina turned and went back in the direction they had come from, hoping to find Sal.

———•·•———

Jenna spotted her first. She was walking toward them out of the shadows, hair and dress disheveled and appearing to be in a daze. "Angelina," she called out, "are you all right?"

Angelina's anger had subsided and she was obviously reflecting on what had just happened. As she walked up, she looked at Jenna with questioning eyes, saying, "Jenna, I think I killed someone."

Putting her arms around her to comfort her, Jenna said, "Come, let's get you back to the ship."

Sal came up and hearing Jenna and taking Angelina's hand, said, "Yes, let's get you back to the ship," and the three started in the direction of the cruise terminal. Marcus had dropped back and was on his cell.

———•·•———

Franco was beside himself. "Adriana, where could they be?" he shouted. "It's past 11:00; everyone is supposed to be onboard." Walking out on the balcony and looking down, he continued, "See, they are stowing the boarding ramps. They are going to miss the ship."

"Calm yourself, Franco. We don't sail until midnight. I trust Sal. I am sure they will be here soon. They always stow the forward ramp when all passengers are supposed to be on board. The aft ramp is last and usually just before sailing time, allowing for the late arrival of crew members."

Just then the cabin phone rang and Adriana, being inside and close to the phone, picked it up, saying, "Hello, Mrs. Gambioni here . . . . Oh, Sal . . . . Thank you. We were worried."

Hanging up and turning to Franco, she continued, "That was Sal. He said they got a little delayed in Old San Juan but are on their way. He notified the ship and they transferred his call to our cabin. See, I told you not to worry. Sal is a good boy. He will take care of us all."

"You are right, Adriana. I get carried away," responded Franco with a slight smile but inwardly thinking, all is not well.

———•—•———

Sitting in bed, Jenna and Marcus began to review the day.

"Jenna, with all the excitement, I didn't get to tell you about my call to headquarters in New York and my discussion with the local FBI. The FBI said the roundup in Manhattan affecting all the Mafia families but the Gambionis was by intent. Primarily because of our mission. They knew this drug deal was going to go down and wanted it to sort out so they would know just which drug cartel was going to try to set up operations in the New York area. By the way, they have no clue as to who was responsible or why Franco's number two was killed. And they were aware of Interpol being involved. The possibility is that the drug connection could go from Colombia to New York or from Colombia to Sicily to New York. The Calisto cartel has been smuggling drugs into Europe quite successfully and the thought is that smuggling drugs into the US by way of Europe might be the possible new route. The Londoño cartel has been concentrating on Florida and Texas as entry points and therefore would like to use Franco as another entry to the US market. Franco doesn't realize it, but he is really the pawn in this operation. The Colombian cartels are still jockeying for market share and the US market is the plum.

"That is all very interesting but what's our involvement now? The ship is on its way back to New York, so how is there any way Franco can have any further meetings with either cartel? So what are we supposed to do? Mind you, I am enjoying the cruise."

"Oh, and how does what happened in Old San Juan fit into the picture?" responded Jenna. "I know they said they would take care of whatever, relative to the attackers," she continued. "By the way, that was an interesting story you told Sal about having a friend locally that had an in with the local police and would take care of everything. What surprised me was that he bought it all. But back to the FBI and our assignment, I am curious."

"It's a little complicated," said Marcus. "They followed Sal and Franco during the day earlier and they did only meet with the Londoños. So one would think that the Londoño/Gambioni link was a done deal. However, the failed kidnapping of Angelina and the reporting that there is a possible Sicilian Mafia family member buried in the crew onboard sets up the possibility that the deal might not be totally set up. Therefore, our assignment is still in effect, that is, keep tabs on the Gambionis and report," continued Marcus as a smile slowly emerged on his face.

As Jenna was about to respond, Marcus turned toward her, snapping off the overhead light. He kissed her playfully on her nose. Jenna tilted her head up slightly, allowing him to kiss her with passion and he whispered in her ear, "I think I'm falling in love with you." He began to lightly brush his fingers along her arm, her cheek, her neck, running downward along the curve of her waist and her hips, then slipping his hand inside her front-buttoned short nightshirt. She turned to him and he continued to gently caress her. Brushing his hand along the skin below her navel, he stroked back up around the curves of her breasts and along her ribs. She responded by pulling his head to her breasts. They made love over and over again, communicating with each other the entire time by touch alone.

I believe I am winning him over, she thought. *I so want him to love me.* Wrapped in each other's arms, they fell fast asleep.

CHAPTER 10

Unsavory Culprits

B reakfast in the Gambioni suite presented a tense family discussion. Two large carafes of coffee and a huge plate of Danish were on the coffee table. Only words of "good morning" had
been uttered by the three between gulps of coffee and bites of
pastry. Angelina set her coffee down and, looking at her father
with a loving but very serious expression, said, "Look, Father,
I know you have been trying to shield me from what you do all
these years. Quite frankly, I have known for some time but I just
didn't want to disappoint you. You probably thought sending me
to Mount Holyoke would also help shield me from the real world
in New York. What you probably didn't know is their prelaw
program offered several courses on crime in the US, including
organized crime. I attended some of the courses and some of the
seminars.

"Angelina! Don't go there," said Franco in a loud, disturbed
voice.

"Father, listen. I know! I also knew that a day would come when
I would have to defend myself as you or someone else assigned
would not be there to defend me. Thank God for my martial arts
training. Well, last night it happened. Luckily, I escaped. I might
have killed someone in the process. I don't know. I don't think I
want to know. Luckily, Marcus has a friend who he said would

take care of things and we got back on the ship before anything else happened. Father, you have to tell me what's going on. Or tell us," looking at Adriana and asking her, "Mother, did or do you not know?"

"Angelina, I thought Sal could protect you."

"Father, I told you what happened. No one could have done any better."

"I am not sure about that, but you are safely onboard and we are on our way back to New York. The next three days you should just relax and enjoy the features of the ship: the pool, the spa. Spend some time with your new friends, the Petersons."

"Father, I need to know."

"Angelina, all you need to know is that Sal and I completed our business in San Juan. Hopefully, you gleaned from your organized crime studies the fact that the less you know, the better off you are."

Angelina bit her lip and, with a frustrated expression, said nothing but got up and left the cabin in a huff.

"Franco, I know you believe you are protecting her by not keeping her informed, but with the Luigi murder we don't know what we will face when we arrive in New York," said Adriana. "You have got to tell her something."

About 300 miles south, a heated discussion went on in Carlos Calisto's cartel headquarters in Cartagena.

"What, are you crazy? The bitch killed Juan and got away," asked the one obviously in command, addressing the group assembled in the dining room of the Calisto penthouse. "She was just a young girl. Two of our best people can't accomplish a simple snatch. What the hell is happening to this organization? I go on a brief trip and nothing that was assigned gets accomplished. You don't convince Gambioni to do business with us when he is here; you fail at putting pressure on him in San Juan by kidnapping his daughter. Carlos will have us all killed. He gave strict orders. Get a piece of the US market. He knows Londoño is doing much better there than we are in Europe and he wants in."

"It's not over!" said one of the group assembled.

———————

Sal was beside himself. He had searched every possible place on board that he could think of where Angelina might go. Franco said she was upset with him and he was concerned where she might go or what she might do. The Sanctuary was the last possibility. This exclusive outdoor spa-inspired deck available for the solitude seekers had appealed to Franco due to the privacy there. Sal was aware that Franco had bought a family access. This just might be where she would go, Sal thought. As he walked through the gated entrance, he was surprised to see the entire sanctuary empty and then she caught his eye. She was lying on a cushioned chaise lounge overlooking the spa pool on the deck below. He almost missed her as she was positioned slightly behind a clump of artificial trees set in the area for atmosphere. As Sal approached, she moved a little and then opened her eyes and, seeing him, let out a soft, "Oh, Sal, how did you get here? Oh, there must have been something in that drink. I passed out." Then looking at the empty cocktail table next to her, she shrieked, "It's gone, my drink is gone." As she began to sit up on the chaise, an envelope fell to the deck. Picking it up, she said, "This must have been placed on me when I was unconscious. It's addressed to my father!"

"Angelina, you must have been drugged. Do you remember who served you the drink?"

"No, not at all. They do it all the time up here. You sit down and someone almost immediately sets a health food drink on your table. I never looked up to see who it was. Actually, I was pretty preoccupied. I had had it out with my father."

"I know, he told me."

"Look, I know he is part of the Mafia. Why can't he be honest with me?"

Sal sat down on the end of the chaise and, looking at Angelina with eyes that definitely transmitted the emotion *I really care for you*, said, "Angelina, if you know that, then you also know that too much knowledge can be dangerous to all concerned. And for your further information, your father is not part of the Mafia, he is the Mafia."

That last comment by Sal caused Angelina's eyes to widen. She also felt a slight twinge in her stomach as she suddenly realized her father must be a Don.

Sal, standing up, scanned the area, then looked back down at Angelina, saying, "There doesn't seem to be anyone else up here. I didn't see any attendants or other passengers when I came in and none has arrived since I have been here. Can you get up? Here, let me help you. Let's get you back to your cabin." Sal took the letter from her and, putting his arm around her in a supporting fashion, helped her up and walked her to the Sanctuary exit.

Carlos Calisto was filled with hate for Pablo Londoño. Sitting in the deserted Oasis Bar, he began reflecting back when they were both lieutenants in the Medellin cartel before its breakup. His thoughts were so strong that the muttering to himself was almost aloud. "*It never failed, no matter what the job, Pablo always seemed to get the credit or was picked first. I or my boys did the killing and he invariably was recognized or got whatever was the prize. It was like the Vázquez brothers didn't know I existed. Pablo was always the front man. Then, after we and some of the other lieutenants started up our cartels, he always was just little ahead of all of us. First to get production back in operation and first to reestablish market contacts. Then he got that damn wife of his. She is as slippery as they come. I am sure she thinks she has wound old Franco around her finger. Well, they are not going to win this one. He may think he has it all with that big yacht he uses for all offshore meetings and operations. Well, he just better be careful; you never know what can happen at sea. I think he probably has forgotten how to get down in the trenches and take on an operation if it needs to be done. If he hasn't forgotten, he still wouldn't have the guts to do it. Well, watch and see with remorse, Pablo. My organization is the best, especially when it comes to doing what might seem impossible, like getting me and four of my boys on this ship. As a bartender, I should be able to accomplish what I need to and my boys, working as cleanup staff in the food court, will always be available if needed. Our food service badges should be able to get us just about anywhere we want. The only issue I have is that I have to work with that greasy wop the Sicilians got on the ship. The stupid ass already caused a problem by attacking one of the crew. The last direct communication I had with Sicily was that they were working the issue in New York. Whatever they are doing, I hope it doesn't screw up Franco's organization as that's what we are depending on for distribution."*

"Excuse me, bartender, are you open? Can I get a drink?" asked a passenger wrapped in a towel walking up to the outside bar and startling Carlos, bringing him back into consciousness of the real world.

———•+•———

Marcus, glancing around seeing expressions on men's faces as they walked by, felt they were filled with envy. Here he sat between two chaise lounges filled with two of the most attractive bikini-clad women in the pool area. Both Jenna and Martina cut beautiful figures. As they chatted in idle conversation, Marcus occasionally applied sun tan lotion where directed.

"I am here on strict orders from the ship's physician. No work for the rest of the cruise, just rest and relaxation," said Martina as one of the staff walked by, recognizing her and questioning her not being in uniform.

Marcus bent down to Martina and, speaking quietly so no passerby would hear, asked, "Were you able to identify the person who attacked you?"

Martina turned her head toward Marcus and said, "No, I mean I couldn't find the person in the ship's crew when I went through the crew pictures with Security Officer Smith. That doesn't mean he is not on board. There are any number of things he could have done when his picture was taken that would have made him unrecognizable to me. I was only basing my original recognition on a mug shot I saw in the Rome office and I only saw him briefly before he knocked me down."

"Well, you better be alert. If it was the person you think it was, I am sure his presence is part of the scheme to get Franco to do business with the Calisto cartel and the Sicilian Mafia," said Marcus.

"Oh, while I was working with Officer Smith, he said he was reviewing the food staff crew members that were boarded in Cartagena and in San Juan."

Hearing this, Jenna turned her head toward Marcus and Martina and said, "I thought he did that on our way to San Juan and I wasn't aware we put on crew in San Juan."

"He did, but he said he had gotten new rosters from HR while in San Juan and was correlating them with the ship's log. There appeared to be a mismatch of names or misspelling or some-thing; he wasn't specific about what he was looking for. And you are right. It wasn't expected but some bar staff was added in San Juan."

In a facetious manner Marcus said, "Well, my lady agents, I believe we may be in for a challenging cruise to New York." Then changing to a serious expression, he added, "Let's hope it is only information gathering and nothing more." Then getting up, Marcus said, "Any one thirsty? I am."

"I would like a beer. I think I have had enough of those sweet rum drinks for awhile," said Jenna.

"Me, too," chimed in Martina.

"Then a bucket of beer it is. In a bucket we pay for four and get five. I'm off," said Marcus.

———•◦•———

A slight breeze came up, sending most of the sun seekers leaving the area of the deck they were occupying. The girls were sitting in the chaise lounges when Marcus got back. Seeing the expression on his face as he came up and set the bucket down on the cocktail table between the chaises, they cried out, "Marcus what's the matter? You look like you saw a ghost."

"I think I have. You are going to have to see this yourselves. I believe the bartender down at the Oasis Bar is a dead ringer for Carlos Calisto. I know drug lords run their operations from their heavily guarded ranchos or, like Pablo, they may have a yacht. But I swear this guy looks just like the pictures we saw of Carlos. I looked at his name badge when I signed for the beers and it wasn't Carlos Calista. I think it said Juan something. I couldn't read it all."

"Well, Calisto does have the reputation of getting out among them. The word back in my office is he has been in Sicily but well protected by the Mafia and never where he could be apprehended. Are you sure it's him?" asked Martina.

"I am not sure how we find out whether he is a look-alike or the real thing, but we better start with Security Officer Smith," said Jenna. "What would a drug lord worth millions be doing as a bartender and be where he could be recognized and possibly apprehended? Give me a break; they have people to do their dirty work," she continued.

"Well, if it isn't a look-alike and it really is him, he has got to be one cocky son of a bitch," said Martina.

———•◦•———

Martina had a difficult time trying to sleep. She lay in her bunk in her small cabin reflecting on the day's activities and the enjoyable evening spent with Marcus and Jenna. They had eaten together, which was good fun and actually a refreshing change from eating in the crew dining area. They were surprised at not seeing the Gambionis.

"They must have either eaten in their room or gone up to the Windows Court," Marcus suggested. Following dinner the three proceeded to bar hop throughout the ship on their way to the showroom. The excuse was the search for the Carlos Calisto double. His discovery never occurred. But their travels provided a pleasurable escape from reality as they witnessed the various entertainments in each of the bar areas.

I loved Jenna's parting comments. I think she said I never knew an agent's life could be so thrilling.. I'm afraid she will find out that there are also down days to the job, thought Martina. In between reflections on the fun evening, her agent training background forced her mind to also reflect on her attacker and the sighting of Carlos Calisto or his double. *Would he be brash enough to personally board the ship. If he did, he probably was not alone. I'm sure he has some of his men with him, one of whom may have been my attacker,* she thought.

————•—•————

The loud knock on the door and the call, "Room Service," startled Adriana, a light sleeper awakened quickly by the noisy intrusion. Trembling, she said, "Franco, wake up. What time did you call for room service? They are at the cabin door and its 4:00 in the morning."

"Adriana, you must be dreaming again. Room service is not due till 7:00. Now get back to sleep," said Franco as he rolled over.

There was a louder knock on the door and another call, "Room Service."

Franco got up and, going to the door, said, "I'll send him on his way. They must have gotten the time wrong on the order."

Angelina called from her bed in the living area, "Father, I'm awake now and will never get back to sleep. If there is coffee and Danish out there, I'm ready."

Franco peered through peephole in the cabin door and saw a room steward holding a tray with what appeared to be two carafes of coffee and two covered plates that probably held the Danish he always ordered for the family's wake-up snack. He didn't recognize the room steward, but that was of no consequence as it usually was a different steward every morning. Opening the door, he was startled as the room steward pushed by him. As the cabin door closed and Franco turned, he was further surprised to see the steward place the tray down on the coffee table and sit down on the chair facing into the room. Then lifting the plate cover, he said, "Señor Gambioni, please sit down."

All eyes stared at the uncovered plate with awe and fright. Lying on the plate in easy access to the steward lay an FN-57 pistol with a silencer attached. This was the current weapon of choice by both cartels and New York organized crime when executing a hit. Franco slowly sat down while the typical hit scenario flashed through his mind. *He and his family could be killed by the intruder, the pistol thrown overboard and the intruder quickly exiting. Since the steward wore the standard food serving gloves, there would be no trace of his involvement.* Not a sound was uttered by any of Franco's family as their eyes moved back and forth between the gun and the room steward's face.

"Let me introduce myself. I am Carlos Calisto and I apologize for not being able to meet with you in Cartagena. I believe we have much to discuss about our future business relationship."

These words now brought meaning to Franco as he quickly reflected on the letter written in Sicilian Italian that Sal gave him the day before. It had stated that he would be contacted by his established future Colombian source. Angelina sat up in her bed (the sitting area sofa by day) and began to inch toward Carlos but stopped. A quick glance at her father revealed him slightly lifting his palm and giving her a stern look that said, don't even think about it.

———••———

Marcus tried to work out his frustration on every exercise machine available in the spa. Jenna never made a move when he woke up and left for the spa. He had gotten very little sleep as he was totally perplexed. He, Jenna and Martina had spent the entire late afternoon and evening looking at photos of the crew on a computer. That, plus making the rounds of every bar on the ship to see if they could spot the man he thought was Carlos Calista. All this was to no avail. "I know it was him," he said out loud as he lifted two 20-pound weights out of the rack and started a bicep exercise.

"Pardon?" said the man exercising next to him.

"Oh, nothing. I'm sorry; I didn't realize I was speaking out loud," responded Marcus. The gentleman moved away and just then the door opened from the exercise class room and a bevy of women exited. The six o'clock zumba class had just finished. Marcus enjoyed watching the parade as he was lifting weights. They appeared to be going in all directions. Some to the tread-mills, some toward the outside pool, some just exiting the spa area. He almost dropped his weights when he saw Angelina coming out among them. She was perspiring from the workout but had a funny look about her, as if she was not really conscious of where she was. She didn't see Marcus right away as she was looking straight ahead towards the exit door. Marcus called out, "Angelina! Are you all right?"

Turning to Marcus, she called out, "Not now," and kept on walking.

Marcus was stunned as she passed through the door. His first thought was that something was terribly wrong.

Jenna sat at their usual table outside the Windows Court on the Lido Deck. The morning sun and cooling breeze was too enjoyable to be missed. Applying butter and jelly to her croissant, she wondered where Marcus was. He usually beat her to breakfast.

Marcus called as he approached the table, "Sorry, I'm a little late. I experienced a strange encounter at the spa this morning."

"Marcus, you didn't wake me when you left for exercise. When did you leave and what did you encounter?"

"Oh! Well, I woke up before the alarm and you were sleeping so soundly I thought you just needed your rest. Rather than waking you or just going back to sleep, I decided to go up and work out. I was really frustrated at not being able to discover any trace of Carlos Calisto, either in our purview of data files or our bar search. I am surer than ever that was him I saw at the bar yesterday, but if he is not in the data base, how did he get on board?"

"Maybe he smuggled himself on board when they were loading all that food in San Juan. Pallets of crated veggies and fruit coupled with large containers of packaged supplies being moved by forklifts set a nice stage for someone trying to sneak on board. The people loading didn't appear to have any particular uniform so it's difficult to distinguish longshoremen from crew. I could be wrong, but it's a possibility. By the way, what was the encounter?"

"It was Angelina. She was in the spa this morning and had a strange look about her. She appeared to try to avoid me and when I called out to her, she yelled, "Not now," and hustled off. "Strange, really strange."

"Oh, Marcus, I see you picked up two croissants. I hope one is for me; you know how much I like them and one is never enough."

"I know, and yes, it's for you so you won't steal half of mine. What could be wrong with Angelina?"

"Oh, I don't think it could be anything serious. We are not making any more stops and will be home tomorrow so it couldn't be anything with her father. She was just probably tired from a heavy workout. I'll call her when we get back to the cabin and see if she wants to go shopping with me. They are having a big sale today."

"Sale? On the ship?"

"Yes, the stores on board usually have periodic sales and especially when they are changing itinerary. This ship sails for Europe after New York so they will be trying to unload the stock they have onboard for the Caribbean."

"Are there any really good . . . ."

The loud chimes interrupted Marcus and the PA began to blare, "Good Morning, everyone. This is the captain speaking. Many of you may have noticed we have made a slight course change. We will be adding an unscheduled port to our cruise, namely Bermuda. We hope to arrive at 17:00 hours and leave at 20:00 hours. The ship is in need of a critical part for one of the side thrusters utilized in the New York port area to minimize the requirement for tug assistance during docking. It is being flown into Bermuda as we speak. We will be berthing at Heritage Wharf. There will not be time for a visit to Hamilton City, but there are some interesting attractions within walking distance of the ship. Please visit the shore excursion desk for further information. We still plan on completing our cruise to New York tomorrow evening as scheduled. Enjoy your day."

"How exciting," said Marcus, "I've never been to Bermuda. Have you?"

"Only as a small girl."

"Oh, there you are," said Martina as she came up to Marcus and Jenna's table, setting down her coffee cup and hitting the table leg with her foot as she sat down. Marcus was quick to grab his plate of eggs and the plate of croissants before they tumbled to the deck.

"Oh, sorry!" said Martina. "Myla said I would find you here. Look, when we couldn't find Calisto in the data bank last night, I had an idea. This morning I went down to the crew's dining area with some copies of the mug shot we had of Carlos Calisto to see if anyone had seen him. I just had to come tell you what I found out."

"Don't keep us in suspense," said Marcus.

"Well, a lot of the bar staff sit together and, since you said he was tending the bar where you got the beer, I thought I would start with them. And you wouldn't believe! I laid the picture down in front of a couple of the staff and right away one said, 'That's Juan Ortega. I just met him yesterday.' His friend sitting across from him replied, 'That's not Juan. I know Juan, that's not him at all.'

"Well, I went back up to Security Officer Smith's office and we looked up Juan Ortega in the data file and he doesn't at all look like Calisto."

"So I did see him," said Marcus. "He is on board posing as a staff member. I wonder where the real Juan Ortega is."

"Well, Security Officer Smith has initiated a search for both," continued Martina. "I wanted you both to know that, with Calisto being on board, there will probably be a meeting with Franco, if it hasn't occurred already."

"And I have a feeling there's going to be another dead body found on the ship by the name of Juan Ortega," interrupted Jenna.

"The body was stuffed between two crates of oranges and had been covered with a burlap bag. It probably wouldn't have been noticed for some time had I not instituted a search," said Security Officer Smith addressing the assembled group in Captain Hempsell's office. The captain had called an emergency staff meeting upon hearing of the discovery.

"I had the ship's doctor examine the body and he believes he was killed by two bullets to the head at fairly close range."

"What is the status of the search for Calisto?" asked the captain.

"The entire crew has been alerted and instructed to contact the bridge at any sighting but not to engage," replied Officer Smith.

"The thought of an armed murderer on board a cruise ship is not a pleasant scenario," responded the captain. "This issue must be resolved as expeditiously as possible, hopefully before docking in Bermuda. The safety of our passengers and crew is paramount and we must do everything possible to mitigate any fear or panic that should arise."

The Portofino Dining Room was filled with passengers looking for that great bargain. The tables were piled high with t-shirts, blouses, jackets, etc. The end-of-cruise sale was in full swing. Security Officer Smith had called Marcus and Jenna to his office after the captain's staff meeting and brought them up to speed. There it was agreed that since the crew was involved in the massive search for Carlos Calisto they should concentrate on shadowing the Gambionis, hopefully discovering if a Calisto contact had been made. Jenna's call to Angelina about the ship's boutique sale set the scene in motion.

Getting off the elevator in the alcove at the entrance to the dining room, Marcus and Jenna were surprised to see Adriana and Angelina waiting for them.

"Wow!" said Marcus as they approached. "You two got down here fast. You could have gone on in. We would have found you."

He was happy to see relaxed expressions on both their faces and mumbled under his breath to Jenna, "I guess you were right."

Speaking loudly so all could hear, Jenna exclaimed, "Marcus, my dear, you must learn that the word 'sale' completely overpowers all other thoughts in a woman's mind."

"Amen to that!" chimed in Adriana and Angelina. "Let's go."

Observing the chaos that appeared to be taking place in the dining room, Marcus excused himself, saying, "Look I'll be out here in the atrium enjoying a coffee; I'm not into clothing sales and definitely not into what's going on in there. It looks like a Black Friday sale at Walmart."

After the morning experience, a knock at the cabin door quickly brought Franco to peer through the peep hole before opening it. Recognizing Sal and opening the door, he said, "Come in. We had a startling experience this morning and I want to brief you on it. The women are off to meet with the Petersons and go to some kind of sale, so we can talk."

Franco's curtness and the serious expression on his face concerned Sal. *Something serious must have happened,* he thought. *I am probably going to get chewed out for not doing my job and preventing whatever it was from happening.*

"Sal, Carlos Calisto visited us at 4:00 this morning."

Oh shit! thought Sal, but then he saw Franco's expression soften as he continued. "Sal, you wouldn't believe. The actions of this Calisto character are totally unthinkable. Here he is, a drug lord worth millions, head of a huge cartel, and he is in my cabin giving me a sales pitch, explaining why I should be doing business with him instead of Pablo Londoño. Oh yes, he got my attention when he arrived at 4:00 in the morning brandishing a FN-57 pistol," said Franco.

"But his manner was far different from what we experienced with his staff in Cartagena. He appeared quite congenial and as he spoke, it was obvious that he assumed all family members are part of the business. He had no qualms about talking drug operations in front of Angelina and Adriana. Quite contrary to how we operate, the Colombians appear not to be aware that we try to keep our immediate families in the dark about our operations. What they don't know, hopefully, can't hurt them. Carlos explained how much better a relationship with his cartel would be. His main point was that he has the capability of smuggling in the product either directly or through Europe, emphasizing that the product would always be available regardless of FBI efforts to stop it."

"That's all very interesting, but I wouldn't jump on an agreement," said Sal. "The rumble among the crew is that they are aware that he is on board and a search is underway. Further, and I couldn't validate this, but there is also a rumor that a crew member has been shot and it's thought that Calisto was responsible. It's not clear whether this emergency stop in Bermuda is connected to it or not."

Franco appeared a little taken back on this news and displayed a surprised look. "Do you think they will find him?"

"I don't know, but even though he slipped on the ship somehow, I don't think getting off undetected will be that easy."

"Well, this is a pretty big ship and I'm sure he is quite resourceful, especially considering his power and wealth. He could buy the ship."

"Well, you have a point there. Say, what are your thoughts about Londoño? You more or less agreed to cut a deal with him."

"Sal, Calisto's parting words to me were 'don't worry about Pablo Londoño. He won't be an issue too much longer.' What he meant by that I don't know but I could imagine. There is no love between these Colombian cartels and wars between them are not out of the question."

———— · ——— · ————

Marcus was on his second cappuccino when Martina found him.

"Marcus, here you are! I called your room. I have been

looking all over for you. Look, MI6 has a facility in the Royal Naval Dockyard. I can get us in there during our port stop at Heritage Wharf. You should be able to place a secure call to your office," said Martina. "I'm sure they would like a status, especially considering the latest developments."

Martina couldn't believe what she witnessed. As she finished speaking, Marcus lit up like a Christmas tree. It appeared that all thoughts of the current situation on board vanished from his mind and his imagination had obviously leaped into high gear. He responded, "Really! MI6, Her Majesty's Secret Service, James Bond!"

"Marcus, calm down. No James Bond, MI6 is no different than your organization. Look, you have the FBI and the CIA. The Brits have MI5 and MI6. They are very similar organizations. Interpol has the same relationship with them as we have with the CIA. In fact, it probably would be good idea to brief them on the caper we have been involved with. I don't know their activities involving drugs. However, I'm sure they would be interested in the Mafia/Colombian drug cartel operations that we have encountered."

Marcus had a glassy-eyed look and his mind was still somewhere else. Visions of James Bond and the beautiful female adversaries were flashing through his thoughts. Martina reached across the table and grabbed both of Marcus's hands, loudly saying, "Marcus, Marcus! Settle down. You didn't hear a word I said."

"What, what. Oh, I'm sorry. I guess I got a little carried away. What about MI6."

Martina reiterated what she had told him and they agreed to meet at the gangway shortly after debarking was announced.

CHAPTER 11

The Bermuda Triangle

It was shortly past noon when Marcus and Jenna returned to their cabin. Their journey through the ship to the sale down in the Portofino Dining Room and the Atrium, where Marcus had coffee with Martina and their return kept them completely within the confines of the ship. They were totally unaware of the outside environment.

Opening the cabin door, Jenna exclaimed, "Marcus, why is it so dark in the cabin?"

"Oh, the room steward must have closed the drapes when he finished cleaning. The afternoon sun on our side of the ship can be very hot."

Entering, they were totally surprised. The drapes were open but there was no light from outside. In fact, there was minimal visibility. Moisture appeared to be streaming down the sliding glass door but they could barely see the balcony furniture or even the balcony railing.

"Marcus, we are in a dense fog. It was bright and sunny this morning when we went down to meet Angelina and her mother. What happened?"

Jenna could see Marcus's face change from his normally relaxed expression to one of almost real fear. He settled in the chair and motioned to her to sit in the couch opposite and then said, "Jenna, have you ever heard of the Bermuda Triangle?"

"Oh, yes," she replied quite cheerfully and with a smiling questioning face continued, "You don't believe all those myths about the triangle, do you?" Then pausing for a moment, her eyes widened and facial expression became very tense. She continued, "Oh, no."

"Oh, yes," said Marcus, "we have been traveling along its eastern border since we left San Juan. Theoretically, the three corners of the triangle are Miami, Bermuda, and San Juan. Strange things have been reported concerning ships and planes traveling in the Bermuda triangle area and they aren't myths. They are well documented. In fact, some ships and planes have been reported to have totally disappeared without a trace."

———•+•———

Through the cold, heavy fog you could barely see the four men standing at the Retreat Bar outside the Sanctuary on the Sun Deck. Carlos Calisto appeared to be addressing one of the four in particular. If you were close enough, you might have heard, "Look, my Sicilian friend. I will be leaving shortly. I believe I've cemented a deal with the Gambioni family so you can tell your people back home and in New York not to do anymore meddling. I will be in contact when shipments commence. That goes for you also. Let me be clear, if you should do otherwise, my boys here might be forced to arrange an unfortunate accident."

———•+•———

It was a tense scene on the bridge of the Golden Duchess. All positions were manned and Captain Hempsell had returned and taken over the watch. The lack of visibility and the four-second fog horn blast every two minutes provided an eerie environment. Captain Hempsell's eyes were glued to the newly installed ECDIS screen. The availability of the Electronic Chart display and Information System was mandatory in 2012 on all passenger ships. It had been incorporated into the Golden Duchess's bridge at its last refit. Displaying documented chart information along with GPS and radar data, the ship's position along with other vessels and landmasses in the vicinity were clearly displayed.

"Hopefully, this new system will give us better awareness of our circumstances," he said to the Officer of the Watch, who was on radar number one. The Junior Officer of the Watch was on radar number two and dealing with phone calls and alarms.

"It appears to be tracking well, sir. I checked it with radar number one before you arrived."

The Junior Officer of the Watch reported, "Captain, we appear to be in a localized condition. The Royal Naval dockyard, some four hours north, reports clear and sunny conditions. They have received no other reports of fog in the area."

"Thank you, Jones," said Captain Hempsell and, turning to Deputy Captain Wardlow, who was filling the Officer of the Watch position, he asked, "What do we know about these vessels appearing behind us and the one southwest of us?" "Sir, that larger vessel to our southwest is the Carnival cruise ship Magic. It's on an easterly course out of Port Canaveral to Bermuda. Jones contacted them earlier and they reported no fog in their surroundings and indicated that they expect to arrive at the Royal Naval Dockyard this evening much later than us. The two immediately behind us have been tracking us since San Juan. They appear to be sizable motor yachts. They are only visible on radar as they stay far behind us. As you can see, they also appear to be quite separated. They may even be far enough apart that they aren't aware of each other's presence."

"Have we . . . Oh, my God," said Captain Hempsell as the bridge cabin lights dimmed and all panel lights and screens went dark.

The Officer of the Watch on the Carnival ship Magic was totally perplexed. He had been staring at the number one radar screen, then quickly looking over at the number two radar screen. He called to the captain saying, "Sir, I don't understand, but the Golden Duchess we were tracking completely dropped off detection on both radars one and two. Seconds before, they were clearly visible and appeared on a northerly course to Bermuda traveling at 26 knots."

"Have you had radio contact with them?" asked the captain.

"Yes, earlier sir. They contacted us and reported they were in a fog. I informed them we were in clear waters and had no evidence of fog in the area."

The electronic fog bank, thought the captain. *This could be evidence that such a thing exists. I've heard about it, The Hutchison theory that the interplay of electromagnetic fields of different wave lengths could cause a grayish metal-like fog. It supposedly could cause all sorts of weird things to happen. I never believed it. There are so many stories and theories about the Devil's triangle.*

"Keep monitoring their last position and trying to make radio contact," commanded the captain and then turning to the Deputy Captain, he said, "Better contact the US Coast Guard and inform them of our observation."

All conversation in the Gambioni cabin ceased. Sal had been talking with Franco about calling New York when they docked in Bermuda. He assumed there would be good cell service there and it would be a good idea to see what the latest was concerning the FBI roundup of Mafia bosses. As Angelina and Adriana returned from shopping, their entering the cabin interrupted the conversation and no sooner had the cabin door closed when all went dark.

"Father, what's happening?" called Angelina.

"It must be a power failure," said Sal, quickly producing a pen flashlight from his pocket and shining it so they didn't trip on the cabin furnishings.

"Oh, my God," cried Adriana as she staggered to the closest chair, dropping her packages from shopping. "I can feel it. The engines have just stopped. We appear to be floating out of control. We are rolling with the wave action of the sea. Do you feel it? It's like there is no stabilization."

"Relax, Adriana," said Franco in a firm but calming voice. "I'm sure there is an explanation."

"Marcus, what's happening?" cried Jenna, throwing her arms out and grabbing Marcus as they tumbled to the bed. In a matter of seconds, the cabin lights went out putting them in complete darkness. All forward motion of the ship appeared to cease causing a feeling of being on a bobbing raft floating aimlessly at sea. This was quickly followed with the feeling that the ship was being lifted and falling as if on a giant wave. The motion had caused their fall.

"Methane hydrates," yelled Marcus.

"What?" cried Jenna, squeezing her hold on Marcus.

"It's sometimes called mud volcanoes, supposedly large quantities of methane gas bubbling up in the sea. It's one of the theories I read about that supposedly could cause the documented disasters that have occurred in the triangle."

Tears began to form in Jenna's eyes as she snuggled closer to Marcus and said, "Marcus, I love you. Are we going to die?"

A large bang brought their eyes to the balcony.

"Oh, my God, we're sinking," said Marcus, seeing nothing but water and their deck furniture banging against the sliding glass door. Sensing the feeling that the ship was moving downward rapidly he staggered over to the wardrobe and grabbed their life-jackets. Jenna screamed. Time seems to move slowly in a crisis.

Seconds seemed like minutes, minutes seemed like hours. The ship began to rise, and then forward motion was felt.

"The ship's under power," cried Marcus.

The cabin lights came on and all felt stable again.

"I think we made it through," said Marcus.

"Through what?" asked Jenna.

"The methane gas bubble area. It could have sunk the ship. I think due to our rapid forward motion before power was lost, and then the speedy restarting of the turbines, we got through. This will go down in history as a Bermuda Triangle disaster avoided."

To date, there has only been one occurrence when such a phenomena has been survived. That was reported to have been with a private plane, not a ship.

CHAPTER 12

Bermuda

Almost on schedule the Golden Duchess slowed to seven knots, allowing for pickup of the pilot from the Royal Naval dockyard. It was clear and the sun was in its last quarter. The sea was calm. Turning to Deputy Captain Wardlow, Captain Hempsell said, "I believe on this ship the voyage data recorder feeds a recording control unit and a data acquisition unit besides the so-called black box, or external protective storage unit, which is sealed. We should be able to access that system and review what was recorded. Considering what we went through, the data may further explain all that happened. Even though reports from staff and crew indicate we only suffered superficial damage, primarily in the Atrium and Promenade Deck areas. Of course, we probably lost a lot of deck furniture from all our balcony cabins. I believe the data could indicate areas to further inspect. In addition to navigation and status of the ship information, it records accelerations and hull stresses."

"Good thought," replied Wardlow. "I'm a little curious about the Echo sounder data. Everything was happening so fast I never did check the depth under the keel readings. It could possibly indicate where the methane gas came from."

"Yes, that would be good to document but theory has it that such occurrences never happen in the same location."

"You are so right about things happening fast. It will be interesting to hear what we were saying and the orders we were giving. Besides the VHF radio communications, the VDR records all audio on the bridge including the bridge wings. It was pretty exciting here for awhile. Frankly, I am amazed we survived what we just experienced. I believe we have to be the first ship to do so."

Franco sat on the one remaining deck chair left on his balcony. As with most of the balconies on his side of the ship, 90 percent of the deck furniture was lost in the incident that they had just experienced. The captain had explained over the PA system that the ship had survived two major Bermuda Triangle occurrences simultaneously. The so-called electric fog bank and the methane bubbles. None of his explanation made much sense to Franco and as far as he was concerned, he was happy to be alive and would definitely never take another cruise. Cell phone in hand and looking up at Sal, who was standing close by, he said, "We have service; it's ringing." And then speaking into the phone, he continued, "Alphonse! Hello . . . . Yes, we are OK . . . . You heard about what happened? . . . All over the news, on TV? So fast. It was just hours ago . . . . I'll tell you all about it when we get home. It really scared the shit out of us. We are coming into Bermuda now."

"No, it wasn't scheduled but the captain announced earlier that we needed some kind of part for the ship's thrusters that are required in New York. He was stopping briefly in Bermuda to pick it up. Then this damn fog and storm hit us. So I assume they will also check the ship over for damage while we are in port there."

"No, originally we were supposed to still arrive tomorrow night in New York. I guess that could change."

"What? You're kidding."

Looking at Sal, he said, "Alphonse says the rumble on the street is I will be arrested as soon as we dock in New York."

Then speaking back into the phone, "What about the other Dons they picked up earlier?

All released? They must have good mouth pieces. Alphonse, you better get prepared. I don't care what it takes, but I don't want to spend any time in some damn jail. *Capisci!*"

Hitting the call-end button, and looking at Sal, he said, "Maybe I shouldn't go home"

———•+•———

The Royal Naval Dockyard is the northeasterly port at the entrance of the Great Sound. It is formed by the islands of a craggy limestone-capped caldera rim that is Bermuda. The port is a considerable distance from Hamilton, the main city located well within the sound. Its location made it the logical port to modify for accommodating large cruise ships. The modification involved the building of a large wharf off the mainland that could accommodate these ships with access being provided by a spur road extending out from the mainland. This created two protected basins, one called the north basin and the other Grassy Bay, furnishing protected marina facilities for yachts and fishing boats. A ferry exists allowing for direct service to Hamilton as an alternate to the long drive around the connected islands of the sound.

Jenna and Marcus's cabin provided a great view of the Royal Naval Dockyard as the ship came alongside the King's wharf. Having just gotten off the phone with Martina, they rushed out on the balcony to watch the docking.

"Look at the TV trailers and antennas," said Jenna. "We must be the news of the day. Look, there's Bernews and ZBM9. According to the info sheet available at the shore excursion desk, they are the prime stations in Bermuda. We all could be famous.

"By the way, Martina said they did a total search of the ship as part of the assessment of damage and there was no Carlos Calisto. If he was here, he disappeared."

Marcus's face turned stern and he answered with an argumentative voice, "Well, he was definitely here; we have the dead body of the staff member he impersonated to validate that, along with other crew members. So get off that kick that he was a figment of my imagination."

Then quickly relaxing and continuing in a pleasanter tone, he said, "They will probably interview Captain Hempsell and anybody else they can grab. They sort of have us all boxed in. You can't get to the North Arm that takes you to the mainland without passing their trucks. I better get down to the gangway as I told Martina I would meet her there as soon as debarking is allowed.

"Jenna, I think it would be wise for you to go with Angelina and Adriana. I don't anticipate any Gambioni cartel contact occurring but the best way to track the family in this stop might be with wife and daughter. Didn't you say they were going to do a little sightseeing and possible shopping?"

"Yes, but that was before the disaster. They may be too shook up to get off the ship now."

"Give her a quick call. I am sure they will be getting off. I'll check with you later by cell." Giving Jenna a quick kiss, Marcus was out the cabin door.

Sweet, thought Jenna. *Are we really becoming a couple. Did I snag him? I so hope so.*

———— ·•· ————

Marcus and Martina rushed past the television cameras and hustled down North Arm Way to get into town as fast as possible. Martina only had a vague idea where the MI6 office was located but wanted to give them a call as soon as they were in the general vicinity to get further directions.

After disembarking, Jenna hung back hoping to catch the

Gambionis as they disembarked. Marcus and Martina quickly disappeared from her sight as they merged into the crowd walking into town. She was startled as Angelina grabbed her arm from behind saying, "Jenna, aren't you going into town?"

"Oh Angelina, yes, I was really hoping to meet up with you. Marcus went off to the Maritime Museum and I'm really not into looking at a bunch of model ships."

"Well, wait just a minute. My folks are coming and I think Sal, too. My father really got shook up with the storm action and all. They say most of the local sites and souvenir shopping is all within walking distance. So come along with us. It should be fun and maybe it will calm my father down. We might have trouble getting him back on the ship."

———•·•———

The MI6 office was located in one of the old Royal Navy office buildings. It was quite close to the Bermuda Maritime Museum. There appeared to be only a few agents on site but they did have secure communication lines to the US. While Martina briefed the MI6 agents on the Mafia/cartel activity they were tracking, Marcus called the CIA office in New York.

Martina's briefing was somewhat stilted because while she spoke to the MI6 agents, she tried to catch as much as she could of Marcus's conversation with the CIA home office.

"Agent Peterson here, sir."

"Yes, we are fine. Surprisingly, the ship appears to have experienced very little damage from the ordeal."

"No, this stop was scheduled before the Bermuda triangle incident."

"We are not sure but we think the Calisto cartel contacted Franco after we left San Juan. It's a little complicated, involving a crew murder and all, but it will all be in my report."

"They are? If Franco gets wind of this, he may try to leave the ship."

"No, I'm in the Bermuda MI6 office but agent Adams is with the Gambioni family. I don't know if Franco got off the ship but I will alert agent Adams. Could Franco get asylum in Bermuda?"

The interviewers from the TV stations became quite aggressive mingling among the crowd with portable microphones and TV cameras. The passengers, many still distressed from the ordeal they had just experienced, were trying to leave the ship and the area as fast as possible. At last dry land, stable footing. Some couldn't wait to tell their story. Others wanted nothing to do with the interviewers. Thus there arose a logjam of people on the North Arm access road. Jenna and Angelina were frantically working their way through the crowd with the Gambionis and Sal in tow.

"We don't have a lot of time," said Jenna, "but we should be able to catch a lunch at the Bone Fish Bar and Grill and get on over to the Bermuda craft market before we have to be back on board. According to the shore excursion desk, the grill is just as we enter the main road from the access road and if we take a right on Maritime Lane, it's a short walk to the craft market."

"I'm not so sure Sal and my father will be that excited to go to the craft market, but I understand there is an art center right next to it. Maybe they will go in there while we shop," responded Angelina.

They were still in the crowd on the access road when Jenna's cell phone vibrated. "I better take this. It must be from Marcus," she said as she put the phone to her ear.

Luckily with the bustling crowd, Angelina didn't notice how serious Jenna's face got as she listened on the phone. Marcus relayed to her the FBI's intentions to arrest Franco as soon as the ship docked in New York and further told her that if Franco knew, he might try to run. Maybe try to get asylum in Bermuda. His final words to her were, don't let Franco out of your sight.

Looking back, Jenna saw both Sal and Franco carrying small bags.

"Oh, shit," she said, and then quickly responding to Marcus, she said, "I'm sorry, yes, I will surely try. We are off to the Bone Fish Bar and Grill and maybe the craft market. Catch you later." Closing the phone and putting it away, she put on a smile for Angelina.

"What was that all about?" asked Angelina.

"Oh, nothing serious. He just said he spilled something on his pants and if I see any spot remover in our travels, I'm to pick it up," said Jenna but her thoughts were, *How do I keep an eye on Franco if he and Sal split off from us, and are they carrying over-night bags?*

While this was going on, no one paid any attention to the two large yachts slowly making their way to moorings in the adjacent North Basin marina. Nor did anyone notice the coffin on a gurney emerging from the forward shell door on Deck Four being loaded into a waiting hearse.

———•—•———

The Bone Fish Bar and Grill had a sizable outdoor seating area. Jenna spotted it initially and motioning all to follow, yelled, "There it is. That place is going to fill up fast, let's go."

"I'm with you on that," said Sal. Grabbing Angelina's arm, he led the troops up on the outside deck of the restaurant. Spotting an empty roundtable for six, Sal caught the head waiter's eye and motioning towards the table, received a nod. They all immediately sat.

"What a great view. You can see the ship and the TV vans in one direction and over to the right the marina. Beautiful!" said Angelina.

Franco appeared to have relaxed a little and, helping Adriana get seated, said, "You are so right, Angelina. After lunch you girls can go shopping and maybe Sal and I will just stay here and watch the world go by."

At that announcement, Jenna's gut twitched and she thought, *Oh, shit, how am I going to watch Franco and go with Angelina and Adriana at the same time? This is getting a little dicey. I can see the ferry dock over by the marina and there is a ferry in port. They could be on it as soon as we left them.*

Her thoughts were immediately shattered when Sal called out, "Holy mackerel, do you see what I see? Look over there," and pointing toward the marina, he continued, "those two huge yachts approaching the marina. Franco, isn't one of them the Londoño yacht?"

"The Reina del Mar? You must mean the farthest one out? The one approaching now is definitely not," said Franco.

"Yes. The farther one. It sure looks like the Reina del Mar."

Playing dumb, Jenna asked, "Who is Londoño? Wasn't the Reina Del Mar the yacht you were going to buy in St. Thomas?"

"Yes, yes. Londoño was the owner," said Franco in a very relaxed ho-hum voice.

Angelina looked over at Sal and rolled her eyes. Jenna's imagination began to spin again.

I wonder if the other yacht is Calisto's. Could both drug lords be here in Bermuda still trying to cut a deal with Franco? If they followed us from San Juan, I wonder if they went through the same Bermuda triangle issues.

The approaching waiter captured the attention of all at the table. Dressed in the classic island attire of Bermuda shorts and knee socks, with a strong Cockney accent he announced,

"Fish and chips with a Pimm's Cup is the special of the day. $20 BMD or US."

"What's a Pimm's cup?" asked Angelina.

Before the waiter could answer, Jenna spoke up, "Oh, you will love it. It's Pimm's #1 liquor and ginger ale. I had it a couple of times when I was traveling with my family. I remember it was so good."

"That sounds a little too sweet for me," said Franco. "I'll be happy with your local beer."

The waiter quickly responded, "That would be the Dockyard brewery; it is close by. We carry their Somers Amber Ale and their Black Anchor Porter. Either goes well with fish and chips."

"That sounds good for . . ." Before Sal could finish the sentence, there was a loud explosion. Looking in the direction of the noise, all saw the huge fireball where the Londoño yacht had been.

"What the hell?" said Carlos. "Why now? You should have accomplished that before you picked me up. Or waited until we were back out at sea. In port here, we could get involved."

"Sorry, sir. The charge was planted onboard back in San Juan. They were never close enough on the trip up to trigger it with our remote," said one of Calisto's men on the bridge of the yacht.

"Well, let's play it right. Radio the port and tell them we will turn and go back toward the explosion to look for survivors. We want them to think we're good sailors. Of course, we will make sure there are none," commanded Carlos.

Pablo had first class seats on his Jet Blue flight from Cartagena so was first off the plane at L. F. Wade International Airport. It was a short walk to the arrivals hall in the terminal and clearing immigration was a piece of cake. Having just a carry-on, he went through customs in a breeze. Heading to the cab stand he wondered how long it would take to travel the 24 miles to the marina at Dockyard. He couldn't wait to be back with his wife on board the Reina del Mar. It had only been a few days since they were together but it had felt like an eternity. He was breaking their basic rule of him never leaving Colombia, but she said if at all possible, he should meet her in Bermuda. She thought Calisto was cutting them out. Before exiting the building, he noticed a large crowd gathered in front of a TV screen showing the local news. Approaching one of the bystanders, he asked, "What going on? Is it something local?"

"Yes, a large yacht blew up outside the Royal Naval Dockyard. The Bernews happened to be out there interviewing passengers on the cruise ship that just docked. Coincidently, one of their portable cameras was pointed in the direction of the explosion when it occurred. They are periodically replaying it on the news channel. Stand by; I'm sure they will show it again."

Looking up at the TV and listening, he heard the broadcaster announce what had happened and then the screen went to the scene. Pablo watched in horror. Color drained from his face. He felt totally devastated as he saw the Reina del Mar explode into a huge fireball.

The loud explosion caused the windows to shake in the old office complex of MI6. After alerting Jenna about Franco, Marcus was back on his call to the CIA home office. The noise and building shake caused him to almost drop the cell.

"There has been an explosion. I'll get back to you," he said as he pressed the end-of-call button. "I believe it's in the marina," said one of the MI6 agents, rushing to the window that overlooked that area.

"I have to check on Jenna and the Gambionis," said Marcus to himself as he ran to the door.

Quickly excusing herself from the agent she was chatting with, Martina almost tripped as she ran to catch Marcus before he left. "I'm sure she's fine and has things under control. I'll stay as I want to check in with my Interpol office."

Then totally unexpected by Marcus, she put her arms around

him, gave him a passionate kiss and with a slight grin said, "Be careful; say hi to your wife." She then quickly turned back to the agent she was speaking to.

Marcus couldn't believe what just happened. One minute his head was filled with anxiety for Jenna's well-being, and next came the unexpected passion offered by Martina. Slightly embarrassed, he said goodbye to the MI6 agents and left the office, literally racing back to the restaurant where he expected Jenna and the Gambionis to be.

What was that all about, he thought as he made his way back to the waterfront. *She came on to me once before, but I thought that then she realized Jenna and I had something going. I have to admit to myself she is one hot number. Under different circumstances, I probably would have jumped in bed with her in a minute. I'm sure she doesn't know how close Jenna and I have become under our newlywed cover. In fact, I'm just beginning to realize it myself. My first thought relative to the explosion in the marina was, is Jenna okay.*

Seeing her, the Gambionis, and Sal all standing on the outside deck of the restaurant staring at the Marina entrance cleared his mind as he raced up the stairs to join them.

———•—•———

Pablo had not moved since he watched the news media repeat of his yacht's explosion. It was almost like he was in another world not hearing anything around where he was standing staring in the direction of the TV. Then he heard the voice of the one person he loved and believed he had just watched die in the explosion.

"Pablo, Pablo," called Señora Londoño.

She's calling me from death, he thought. *God, she is in your hands,* he said to himself.

"Pablo, Pablo!" called Señora Londoño again as she made her way through the crowd of passengers watching the TV.

This time Pablo turned toward the sound and could not believe his eyes. There was his wife running toward him. Grabbing her in an embrace, he hardly heard the words she so rapidly was saying, "I'm so glad I caught you. I had scheduled my flight from San Juan to arrive just with yours. I had hoped to surprise you. You know my superstition about the Bermuda triangle. Well, I sent the yacht up with the crew and Ricardo and I flew. He's getting our bags now."

Breaking their embrace and turning the señora toward the TV, Pablo said, "Slow down, watch and listen."

The announcer was again reporting on the explosion that had occurred at the entrance to the Dockyard Marina, showing a repeat of the actual explosion. Then the screen showed the location now. They obviously were continuing to video the area. He announced that another arriving yacht was going back to the area to search for survivors. As the yacht came into view, Señora Londoño screamed, "That *hijueputa*! That's Calisto's boat. I bet that *malparido* is responsible. He will pay!"

"He probably thought you were on our boat," said Pablo. "He will die."

———•◆•———

Jenna was beside herself. Immediately following the explosion Sal and the Gambionis erupted into loud conversation and violent hand gestures, speaking among themselves in Italian. She couldn't understand a word they were saying except the names Londoño and Calisto. By the expressions on their faces and their loud dialogue, they were obviously upset.

"What's the matter? You didn't buy the boat. I don't understand," she said. But they paid no attention to her. She suspected she knew what they were discussing but couldn't blow her cover by saying anything.

Spotting Marcus running towards them gave her a little relief. *Thank God,* she thought. *Hopefully you will be able to bring some order to this chaos.* Little did she expect what would happen next.

———•◦•———

Marcus had no sooner left than the MI6 agent that Martina was speaking to ushered her into an inner office. Martina was amazed. The inner office was very similar to the Interpol office in Cartagena. A small conference table in the middle had speakerphone units on top and two walls covered with video screens depicting many of the areas around the Royal Naval dockyard. She became wide-eyed and the escorting agent saw her surprise and said, "Agent Bufalino."

"Martina, please," she responded.

"Martina, then. You are obviously surprised at our surveillance capability here in the dockyard. Please, let me explain. It is partially for our business but also this facility provides an ideal locale to test systems that we wish to employ elsewhere. It's remote, and has a minimum caseload, nowhere near the size attributed to the MI6 offices in the UK. The current capability that you see allows us to monitor almost 90 percent of the cruise ship traffic arriving here in Bermuda and the tourist traffic arriving at the airport. It includes surveillance cameras in many of the restaurants and sightseeing venues around the dockyard. Look over on screen two. You can see agent Peterson walking towards the restaurants on the pier."

Martina looked at that screen and then some of the others and responded, "There are the Gambionis and Sal and Jenna. That must be at the Bone Fish Bar and Grill."

"It is."

"You don't have any pointed where the explosion was, do you?"

"Well, yes and no. Obviously you would be able to see the port entry through the cameras that are looking at your cruise ship if the ship were not in port."

Briefly grabbing Martina's arm to get her attention, MI6 Agent Taylor continued, "Look, I took the liberty to contact our home office when you called and said you were coming. It turns out that the FBI in the US has contacted us in their endeavor to determine who is behind the drug flow into the US from Europe. MI5 has not made us aware of any drug traffic existing in the UK. However, we have been working with them concerning possible drugs coming in from Europe as opposed to directly from Colombia. If this is being orchestrated by the Sicilian Mafia, we want to be aware. As such, I would like to be party to your call to Interpol headquarters."

"Most certainly. Let's make the call," replied Martina.

"I'll initiate the call with my office in Rome and I'm sure they will make it a conference call with Interpol headquarters in Lyon."

Luckily, even considering the time differences, it was early enough that the offices in France and Italy were still open.

Martina opened the discussion, briefing everyone on the status of all concerned, that is, Franco Gambioni and his contacts with the Londoño and Calisto cartels, as well as the CIA agents Peterson and Adams, who were assigned to watch the Gambionis and report on who they contacted. She included the murdered ship crew member suspected of being of Calisto's doing.

"Bermuda, this is Lyon." Rather than using agent names, locations were used in the telecom. "We have been informed by Cartagena that the Calisto and Londoño yachts left shortly after the Golden Duchess set sail for San Juan."

"Bermuda here, we were aware of the Londoño yacht in San Juan," said Martina.

"We weren't aware that the Calisto cartel had a yacht and also was tracking our ship," she continued. "That could explain the two yachts that were observed approaching the Naval dockyard shortly after we docked."

At that point another MI6 agent entered the room and slid a note to Martina that said the recent explosion was one of the yachts blowing up. "Sir, I've just been advised that one of the approaching yachts blew up outside the harbor."

"It would be interesting to know whose yacht blew up and who was on board. From your report, Carlos Calisto could have been picked up by his yacht if he had jumped ship. The Londoño yacht, we are never sure. Seldom does Pablo ever leave Colombia and Señora Londoño sometimes stays on board and sometimes arranges to meet the yacht, depending on the ports."

That comment was almost a trigger to what happened next. The rim of one of the surveillance camera screens started to flash bright red.

"What does that mean? Is there something wrong?" asked Martina.

"No, not at all. We may be getting more information than we expected from surveillance. The software that drives the system allows us to preprogram pictures of people we want to be aware of if they arrive here in Bermuda. If there is an international warrant, we will hold them for extradition. If they are in the international criminal category but there is no legal warrant for their arrest, we do not allow them to stay. If by air, they are held at the airport till they can get a returning flight. If by cruise ship, they are required to reboard, but this seldom happens as the list of unacceptable visitors is always transmitted to cruise lines so they know in advance if there is anyone on board who is not welcome. Of course, this becomes a little dicey when a ship such as yours arrives unscheduled."

"What about arriving yachts?"

"We depend on the Harbor Patrol to spot any entry that way. We do have a watch list of wanted international criminals who are known to own yachts, and we keep the patrol aware of any changes in the list as it occurs. If someone arrives in that category, they are escorted to the fuel dock and directed to sail on."

"Lyon here. We had no idea that the UK's MI6 had such an operation in Bermuda. Thank you for making us aware. We will certainly keep that capability in mind for any future operations that should occur in that area. Have you gotten recognition on the flashing surveillance screen yet?"

The screen stopped flashing and a solid red border appeared surrounding a picture of a very attractive Hispanic couple.

"Lyon, you called that right," said MI6 Agent Taylor. "The Londoños have arrived at the Bermuda airport. They will be in for a surprise when they find they have no yacht to board. I am sure we can assume the yacht that blew up was theirs."

———————

Jenna could not believe what was happening. Though running, Marcus was still some distance away. The screaming in Italian among the Gambionis and Sal suddenly stopped. Franco and Sal stood up, and picked up the small bags they had brought with them. Franco bent down and kissed Adriana, Sal caressed Angelina's shoulder, and they both left.

"What's going on?" asked Jenna looking at Angelina and Adriana. "Where are they going?"

"They are running to catch the ferry to Hamilton," said Angelina.

"They can't do that. If they go to Hamilton on the ferry, they won't be able to get back before the ship sails. Don't they know that?"

"Yes, they expected that. That's why they're carrying small bags." replied Angelina. "If they miss the ship, they will fly home. It's not a long flight."

"Is that legal? Can they do that?" said Jenna, thinking, *Franco must've found out that the FBI was going to arrest him when the ship arrives. He is going to try and avoid that by staying in Bermuda. We have to stop this.*

Just then, Marcus came running up the steps of the restaurant's deck and, seeing Sal and Franco missing, called out, "Where did they go?"

"They are off to Hamilton on the ferry," cried Jenna.

"Call Martina," Marcus called back as he changed direction and ran towards the ferry.

"You newlyweds shouldn't be worrying about my father and Sal. They can take care of themselves," said Angelina.

She should know, thought Jenna as she said, "Oh, that's just Marcus's nature. He worries about everybody. I'll give Martina a call as a shore excursion person. I'm sure she'll know if there is a problem and what to do."

———·•·———

When Marcus arrived at the dock, the ferry had already left and was headed toward the marina entrance, about 100 yards out. Sal and Franco were on the aft deck and seeing Marcus, they smiled and waved. Waving back, his thoughts were, *Oh shit, what do I do now?*

He was surprised when someone put a hand on his shoulder and turning, he saw MI6 Agent Taylor who said, "Not to worry, we will take it from here. Go back and join your group. I assure you Franco Gambioni and Sal Indelicato will be on the ship when you sail tonight."

———·•·———

Ricardo, wheeling a luggage cart with two small bags, approached the Londoños and seeing the distraught look on both their faces, said, "Señora what is the matter?"

As Pablo explained the yacht situation, Señora Londoño, looking past Ricardo, spotted four airport security officers coming their way. Placing her hand on Pablo's shoulder, she said, "I believe we are about to have a welcoming committee and I don't think they are pleased with our presence."

Pablo and Ricardo immediately looked up and, seeing the approaching officers, Pablo said, "I think we have a problem."

———·•·———

The Calisto yacht slowly circled the area where the Londoño yacht exploded looking for possible survivors among the floating debris.

"There appear to be no survivors and I would have expected a lot more debris," said Carlos.

"The charge was placed below the floorboards in the main cabin. In addition to destroying the yacht proper, it would've blown a hole in the hull well below the water line causing it to sink immediately," said one of his crewmembers.

The sound of a siren got Carlos's attention. Looking up he saw a fire boat and a harbor patrol cruiser heading directly their way. "I am going below deck," he said. "I think we have an issue."

———————

Martina's mind began to spin as she left the MI6 office headed back to the ship. *We really don't know whether Franco cut a deal with either Pablo Londoño or Carlos Calisto. And there's still that Sicilian Mafioso buried in the crew who tried to kill me and who we haven't been able to identify.*

It's really not clear what our next move should be. In 24 hours we will be docked in New York. I'm sure the cruise line will be happy to see us go. Having to deal with two murdered crew members and a seized murderer certainly wasn't expected and keeping it from the cruise passengers presented a major issue for them. My hat goes off to the captain and his staff.

Martina had not quite reached the ship when she was approached by Security Officer Smith. "Martina, I'm glad I caught you. The captain would like a briefing on the status of things and the results of your call to Interpol."

"Good, let's go. There is an issue with the Gambionis that he should know about. MI6 will be taking care of it but it could affect your sailing time."

———————

It had been a long and frustrating day for Marcus and Jenna. First came Marcus's uncompleted call to CIA headquarters in New York, and then Franco and Sal slipping off to Hamilton on the Bermuda ferry. Finally, they had had to complete a lunch with Adriana and Angelina in their undercover persona as newlyweds, all while trying to figure out what their next move should be on their basic assignment: Did the Gambionis establish a drug cartel connection? If so, how and who with?

They made their way back to the ship and to their suite. They literally stripped the clothes off each other, leaping into bed and into each other's arms. As opposed to soft loving tenderness, it was frenzy sex driven by bodily need, a major effort to drown frustration with physical gratification. This continued over and over again until they both fell asleep totally exhausted.

As the ship's horn sounded, they both woke up with a start. "We must be sailing," said Jenna.

They grabbed their robes and ran out on the balcony. The main gangways had already been pulled and most lines had been released, leaving just one bow and one stern line. Then came the *whup-whup-whup-whup* of a large helicopter as it prepared to land on the dock. They weren't surprised when the helicopter door opened and Franco and Sal, escorted by a Bermuda police officer, made their way to the one remaining gangway.

CHAPTER 13

The Eventful Cruise Home

Recognizing they had slept the afternoon away and the ship was underway to New York, Marcus and Jenna busied themselves with getting ready for dinner. Believing he heard a knock on the cabin door, Marcus opened it and was surprised to see a huge amount of paper work stuffed in their cabin mailbox and a cabin steward racing down the hall with an armload of mail. He shouted back to Jenna, "Jenna! Our mailbox is loaded." "That's to be expected, Marcus," she responded. "It's the end of the cruise, and our last night on board. They have to get us ready to get off and they want to say goodbye. It's exciting. You'll see. Bring it all in and we will go over it. There should be disembarkation instructions with baggage tags. We probably will have to have our bags packed and out of our cabin in time for them to be assembled for disembarkation. It's usually by midnight but since we had the unscheduled stop and we are not due into New York until late tomorrow, they could delay it a bit.

"Much of this mail would have been sent out sooner but due to all that's happened, it was probably delayed. There could be an invitation to the captain's reception in there. Our status on board qualifies us for that. I wonder if they will schedule the Champagne waterfall. Oh, I believe they might have the march of the baked Alaska in the dining room. Marcus, hurry, bring it in."

Nothing was said by anyone when Franco entered the cabin as the ship got underway. Angelina and Adriana were dressing for dinner and initially thought it best not to comment to him about the upset of his plan to avoid arrest in New York.

Franco put his bag down and also silently started to dress for dinner when in a very cool voice, Angelina said, "Father, I know you are concerned, but be assured. I am confident that Alphonse will have prepared for the situation. If you are arrested, he will have you out in no time. Remember, all the other Dons who were arrested have been released."

Franco was startled by Angelina's comments. It was as if she were an operating part of the Mafia family. Women were just not allowed in that role. They were kept shielded from all operations for their own safety and so they could not be questioned by the law.

"Angelina, please, you should not be aware or concern yourself."

Angelina turned and faced her father directly and, with a stern and serious face, continued, "Father, one thing we have all learned on this trip is that women can be a major factor in Colombian drug cartels. Maybe the Italian Mafia are missing something. You may not like my desires, but I intend to assist you in running our family. Remember, I have spent considerable time studying organized crime in college. I am physically strong and totally capable of protecting myself. Father, I have killed."

Franco could not believe what he was hearing. This was a daughter he was not aware existed. He looked across the cabin at Adriana and only saw a blank stare as if she also were totally surprised. Trying to possibly lighten the conversation, he asked, "Angelina, what about Sal?"

"Father, he is nice but he is in our employ. I personally consider him a toy. Nothing more."

Franco and Adriana were further overwhelmed with this statement. What kind of offspring had they raised? This beautiful innocent daughter suddenly appeared as cold as nails.

———•+•———

Sal sat in the International Café sipping a latte. He sat at the same table he had shared so long ago on the cruise with Angelina. He recalled that then she was having a difficult time with her relationship with her father. He had tried to make her understand that it was her father's concern for her safety that caused him to be so cold when she questioned him about his business. *How many things had transpired since then,* he thought. *I really began to think she could be in my life. Now, I'm not sure. Marcus was right. You should never consider an involvement with your employer's family.*

"*Buona sera,* Sal. May I join you?" said the soft-spoken Martina, startling Sal as she walked up to his table. He quickly jumped up, saying, "By all means, please do."

His thoughts were instantly racing. *She is certainly the Italian temptress. I recall her moves on Marcus. She could be fun. Maybe that personality is required by cruise staff.*

"Are you off duty?" he continued as they both sat down.

"*Si,* shore excursions are over. I pretty much have my time to myself," she said while thinking, *Maybe if I can get close to Sal, I can find out whether a drug deal was consummated.*

———•+•———

Marcus could not believe the reception line queue for the captain's party. The line in front of the Cabaret Lounge entrance was huge. It seemed to be the length of the ship. "Jenna, why do we have to stand in line? Can't we just go in? . . . . The line, it's moving so slowly, what's going on?"

"Marcus, you don't understand. It's no different than the welcoming reception the first night out on the cruise. You have the invitation, don't you?" Marcus nodded yes and Jenna continued, "Look, Myla will probably be at the door. She will take your invitation and introduce you to the deputy captain who will introduce you to the captain and a photographer will take your picture."

"I already know the captain."

"I know, Marcus. It's just the process. We thank him for a great cruise. Our picture gets taken shaking his hand and we then proceed into the lounge for cocktails and hors d'oeuvres. After everyone gets in, there will be a small program. The captain will say a few words and they will award a prize and probably a bottle of Champagne to the passenger or the couple who have cruised the most days on the cruise line."

The line moved along and Marcus and Jenna approached Myla. As he handed her the invitation, he was surprised as Myla bent close to him and whispered into his ear before announcing them as Mr. and Mrs. Peterson. "When you get inside, go to the far end of the bar. You will see Martina there. She has some important info to pass on to you," she whispered.

The Portofino Dining Room was awash with black, silver and white streamers. It was almost like New Year's Eve. The waiting staff was all dressed in tuxedo uniforms and show tunes could be heard coming softly from the sound system. The evening had been billed as a salute to Broadway.

"Oh, Marcus, this is going to be so much fun," Jenna said as they entered. To their surprise, they were escorted to the Gambioni table as opposed to their own. As they approached, Franco stood up, saying, "Welcome, I took the liberty to have you join us. It's Broadway night and you newlyweds should definitely eat with us. Besides, we have had so much fun together on the cruise. It's only fitting that we eat together this last evening. Please sit."

Knowing what they now knew, it was hard for Marcus and Jenna to comprehend the obvious festive mood the Gambionis and Sal appeared to be in. *How can they be so happy knowing what will probably happen when they arrive in New York. I just don't understand,* Marcus thought.

The table conversation continued to be light throughout the meal, primarily discussions of past events that were shared by all on the cruise. The march of the baked Alaska had occurred but strains of New York, New York, It's a Wonderful Town that the waiters had marched to still lingered in everyone's ears. All at the table had finished their baked Alaska and were sipping their limoncello and coffee when Franco said, "You newlyweds, the honeymoon is just about over. Where do you plan to live?"

The question caught Marcus and Jenna completely off guard. Stammering, Marcus replied, "That really hasn't been decided. We hoped to be in Manhattan but frankly we haven't found a place we can afford. I have a small studio and we will probably stay there until we can find a place. It will be a little tight but we will manage."

"Preposterous!" said Franco. "Look, I have a condominium in the Trump Towers on the west side. It's completely furnished and we keep it for visiting business partners. We currently aren't using it and you're welcome to it while you look for a place of your own."

Marcus displayed a questioning look at Jenna and only saw a blank stare in response. Not wanting the conversation to stall, he said, "Mr. Gambioni, that's such a wonderful offer. I am really not sure we could accept it but we will certainly give it considerable thought."

Saying those words his thoughts were, *Franco, you should only know we're really not married. We work for the CIA and I don't think our boss would like us staying in a condo owned by the Mafia.*

"What's to think about. You need a place, I have a place, you use."

The words were almost like a command coming from Franco. Marcus again looked at Jenna with questioning eyes and the strong thought, *What do we do now?*

To Marcus's relief, Jenna jumped into the conversation. "Oh, Mr. Gambioni. That offer is wonderful."

Looking over at Marcus with a smile, Jenna continued, "The thinking is over, we would be delighted to use it. I'm sure we won't stay too long. We only just started looking before we left on the cruise."

Marcus gasped as he heard Jenna. Looking at her with an astonished expression, his thoughts were, *Jenna, are you out of your mind? What are you thinking?*

Franco, on the other hand, smiled and said, "Marcus, you will learn there are some decisions best left to the wife."

It was well past midnight when Marcus and Jenna left the Gambionis and Sal. They all had gone on to the Duchess Theatre following dinner to see the closing show. Arriving at their cabin, another full mail box greeted them. Their onboard cruise bill and further disembarkation instructions were included in the stack. Marcus grabbed the cruise bill while Jenna quickly scanned the final disembarkation instructions.

"Marcus, we have to have our bags out of our cabin by 10:00. We obviously can't sleep in. Packing can be an issue," said Jenna.

Marcus, thumbing through the cruise bill, responded, "Jenna, my gosh. I had no idea we ran up such a bill. I hope we get reimbursed. This will max out my credit card." Then looking over at Jenna with a stern expression, he continued, "By the way, just what did you have in mind when you accepted Franco's offer? You know there is no way in hell we can do that. It could expose our cover. The office definitely wouldn't approve. What were you thinking?"

"Marcus, listen, our cover could've been blown if we refused.

Think a little, there are some possibilities here. The FBI may not know about this condo and with us staying there, maybe they can wire it."

"Jenna, I am sure the home office would not condone it. Nor would the FBI. Stateside surveillance is strictly the FBI, not the CIA."

While trying to convince Marcus that this was a good thing, Jenna continued to think, *Living together longer than just the 12-day cruise could possibly, hopefully, mature our relationship.*

Jenna was sound asleep when Marcus crept out of bed and, donning his exercise clothes, crept off to the fitness center. *I'm really going to miss this,* he thought. *It's like having a full gym in your own home.*

Getting off the elevator on Deck 16 he ran right into Angelina, who had just gotten off the adjacent elevator. Before he could say a word, Angelina said, "Hi, Marcus, good morning, got to run; I'm late for my class." And with that she was off to the exercise room in the fitness center.

Marcus didn't get a word in edgewise other than a quick, "Hi." *So much for my silent crush on Angelina,* he thought. *Well, a relationship with a Mafia Don's daughter probably wouldn't have been so good for an aspiring CIA agent and I'm really getting to like Jenna quite a bit. Of course, a work-related relationship might not be acceptable either. Hopefully, exercising will clear my mind.*

Marcus headed toward the Windows Court table he usually shared with Jenna for breakfast. He hadn't bothered to call her as he knew she would probably join him. During the course of the cruise sometimes she even arrived before he finished exercising, but not today.

He had just set his coffee and breakfast plate down when he

was startled by a voice from behind. "Myla told me I'd find you here. May I join you?" said Martina.

"By all means, what a surprise. What brings you here so early?" said Marcus, turning to face Martina.

"You know, the ship leaves for Europe tomorrow. Part of my shore excursion job requires me to assist the others on my team. Most of the day before we dock, we will be giving shore excursion overviews in the Duchess Theatre. We will cover all the ports that will be visited during the next cruise. I wanted to see you for some parting conversation and a proper goodbye. I figured this was the best way to do it." Saying that, she put her arms around him, and gave him a passionate kiss.

Oh, oh, here we go again, thought Marcus. *It's a good thing Jenna isn't here.*

Sitting down, Martina continued, "Marcus, I know there are several CIA projects going on in Europe. Some may even be in Italy. You should try to get assigned to one. I would just love to show you Sicily. We could have a great time."

Seeing the sparkle in Martina's eyes as she said those words, Marcus thought, *Oh, I bet we would. How did I get so lucky to have two women hot for me?*

"Martina, that does sound exciting, but this was our first field assignment. I have no idea what I will be assigned to next. I haven't worked with Jenna before, so I have no idea whether they just teamed us up for this assignment and our futures will be in different directions. Maybe we will remain as a team. I really don't know what the future holds."

As he said these words, he could see the sparkle fade from Martina's eyes. It was about then that Jenna arrived and quickly commandeered their attention, saying, "Martina, what a pleasant surprise." Then turning to Marcus, she continued, "Marcus, I packed most of your things but you have to finish up. We only have about an hour and a half before our bags should be out of the cabin in our passageway to be picked up for disembarkation."

"Boy, you two are really into your role-playing. You sound like a real married couple," said Martina.

"Well, after 12 days, it almost feels that way," replied Jenna.

With a serious expression, Martina looked at both Marcus and Jenna and said, "Well, I think we can say that we completed our mutual assignments. As I mentioned at the captain's reception, it's pretty clear that Franco cut a deal with Carlos Calisto. In fact, I got Sal to verify that. That pretty much completes your assignment. I, on the other hand, have further work to do in determining just how the Sicilian Mafia fits into the picture."

Then looking at her watch, she stood up and said, "I've got to get to the Duchess Theatre. It's been great working with you two. I really hope we meet again someday."

Both Marcus and Jenna stood up and Martina gave Jenna a hug and then put her arms around Marcus, giving him another passionate kiss. Then quickly turning, she walked off.

With fire in her eyes, Jenna looked at Marcus and said, "What was that all about?"

Adriana and Angelina returned to the Gambioni suite after their usual breakfast at Raffaello's, still feeling the glow from the multiple mimosas they usually indulged in. Entering the cabin, Angelina's first words were, "Father, regardless of your reason, I really have enjoyed the cruise and these breakfasts at Raffaello's have been wonderful. Meeting mother there after I exercise has been a pleasure. Thank you so much."

"I'm sure the mimosas helped for that to be true," replied Franco with a sly smile on his face. Franco had finished his frittata, which was always delivered precisely at 9:00. Though the cabin balcony door was open, the aroma of garlic was still strong in the room. The basket of *biscottate* and croissants, along with a plate of apricot marmalade routinely delivered with Franco's breakfast, drew both Angelina and Adriana to the coffee table for a second cup of Italian coffee.

Sitting down, Adriana said, "Franco, enjoy, but don't expect this every morning at home." Franco just laughed.

Stirring her coffee, Angelina looked at Franco with a questioning expression, saying,

"Father, what made you decide to offer our Trump condo to the Petersons? When I asked to use it for my friends from college, you told me it had to remain available as you never knew when a business associate might come to town and need it."

Franco's expression quickly flashed to rage, then slowly returned to normal as he said,

"I normally would not share this with you as it concerns family business, but since you were involved during the happening, I will make an exception. Ladies, you are in for a surprise. If you recall, I may have mentioned that on the last call with Alphonse, he indicated that the rumble on the street was we were being watched and information about our whereabouts during the cruise was being reported to the FBI. At that time they had no indication of who was doing the watching or how it was being accomplished. Well, on my call to him last night, he revealed the information he had received concerning our watchers."

Both Adriana and Angelina suddenly stopped what they were doing and gave Franco their total attention. "Ladies, it turns out that our newly-made friends the Petersons are not really who you think they are."

Adriana gasped and Angelina said, "Oh, no."

"Oh, yes," continued Franco. "It turns out they are CIA agents posing as a young couple on a honeymoon assigned to watch our every activity and report same to the FBI. Since the cruise is over, I have elected not to confront them now, and I implore you both to do the same. I have not informed Sal either. Retribution is a family requirement."

Saying these words, his expression returned to anger. "They

will have a fatal experience upon moving into Trump Towers. It turns out the condo will experience a major gas leak and a severe explosion will occur when they enter and turn on the lights. Accidents happen. I'm sure the facility is insured."

Color drained from both women's faces and Angelina said, "Oh, Father, you wouldn't!"

"That is the family way. It has already been ordered," responded Franco.

CHAPTER 14

Disembarkation

The Gambioni family were all out on the balcony of their suite as the Golden Duchess steamed into New York harbor. As they passed the Statue of Liberty, Franco said, "My father used to tell me how impressed he was when he saw that statue. He was a young boy at the time, traveling with his uncle who came over from Sicily to be an underboss of his cousin's family."

"Then I'm just a third-generation Italian-American," said Angelina.

"Well, yes and no. Your mother's family goes back four generations, and is not from Sicily. Her family came from Roma."

"Did she know she was marrying into La Cosa Nostra?"

"I had no idea what your father did," interrupted Adriana. "He was a handsome young Italian boy who swept me off my feet. I don't think I really found out until after you were born. One of his friends was killed and another wife told me at the funeral. It was only then that I asked him what was going on."

"Yes, and I told you then and I tell you both now. It is best that you don't know anything about the business," chimed in Franco. "It can only hurt you and maybe me if you're forced to testify," he continued.

Color drained from Angelina's face, and her hands tightened

on the balcony rail she was holding. With a very stern look, she said, "As I said before, Father, that may change."

"Angelina, hear me now. The Italian Mafia is not a Colombian cartel. Women are not a part of the business organization. You would never be accepted."

"Father, this is the twenty-first century; women are everywhere. Let me assure you that will include organized crime. There are new avenues of revenue to be exploited. This will involve educated members, both male and female. Further, Father, you will find there is no limit on how ruthless women can be."

The Golden Duchess was safely secured at Pier 88 on the Hudson River. The cruise terminal is located at West 52nd street in Manhattan. Disembarkation commenced precisely at 6:00 pm as predicted by the captain. All passengers proceeded through immigration first, then baggage claim and finally customs. Passengers were required to vacate their cabins by 4:00 pm to allow them to be serviced for the next cruise. They were then assigned different waiting areas on the ship pending the calling of their disembarkation number.

Marcus and Jenna were in the Voyagers Lounge waiting to be called. Suite passengers were assigned to the Contessa Grill. "We obviously won't be disembarking with the Gambionis. Where do you think Franco will be arrested?" asked Jenna.

"I would guess at immigration. Officially he is not in the US until he clears there and that's the first desk we approach in the terminal building."

"We probably won't be able to witness it as they will precede us, but we may see them in baggage claim. There we will see if Adriana and Angelina are alone or with Franco."

"That could be interesting. What do we say to them if they are alone? And by the way, on your last call to the office, did they say whether they were sending a car to pick us up or do we have to get our own rides home?"

"Since we are both local, they said to get cabs home and put it on the expense report."

Then with a big smile on his face, Marcus continued, "That brings up another issue. Inasmuch as you accepted Franco's offer, when do we move into our new digs?"

"Well, Angelina gave me the address and said to call her when we are ready and she would meet us there. It's really close by. Trump Towers West is just a little ways north of here. With Franco being arrested, I wonder if the offer is still relevant."

⸻

After clearing immigration, they were directed to the elevators in the cruise terminal that took them to the ground floor. Exiting the elevators, Marcus said, "Jenna, where are we? How does this work? When we boarded the cruise, everything was on the upper floors."

They appeared to be at the end of a long hall filled with passengers and porters coming and going. Jenna, with a wide-eyed expression on her face as she surveyed the area, said, "Oh my, some things never change. This is exactly like it was when I sailed with my folks. This long hall we are in goes by several large bays and you will see all the luggage is there. Our disembarking color and number should be displayed above the bay door where our luggage will be. I suspect it will be in the same bay as the Gambionis as they are usually unloaded by deck and maybe two decks to a bay. At the far end of the hall is customs. They rarely question what you put on the customs declaration form so passengers proceed through rapidly. Behind customs will be exits to ground transportation. That's where we can pick up a cab."

The bay containing their luggage was crowded with passengers and porters scurrying around the laid-out suitcases searching for their own.

"There they are, Marcus, over in the far corner. That wide red ribbon I attached to the handle sure made it easy to spot them."

They were partway across the bay, walking toward their bags, when they heard Angelina's voice, "Jenna, over here!"

In their rush to claim their luggage, they had literally walked past Adriana and Angelina, who were negotiating with a porter just inside the bay door. There was no sign of Franco. Surprised, they turned and walked back to Angelina, who appeared totally relaxed and in control, certainly not what they would have thought of one who had just experienced the arresting of her father.

"I am so glad to catch you," Angelina continued. "Since we are not using the condo, my father wanted me to give you the key so you could go to it at your leisure. Just give me a call when you actually move in. Oh, by the way, since the condo faces west looking over the Hudson river, the afternoon sun is pretty severe so we keep the drapes closed when it's vacant. The light switch is right inside the door as you enter."

The end

Epilogue

Franco Gambioni is serving a term in prison, convicted of extortion and racketeering. Alphonse Romano is in the process of filing an appeal.

To Franco's surprise, the four other Mafia bosses of the New York Commission of the Five Families accepted Angelina as temporary Don of the Gambioni family.

Sal Indelicato's employment by Franco was terminated immediately following the cruise and he subsequently died in a questionable automobile accident.

Jenna is still recovering from injuries sustained in the reported accidental explosion that occurred when she entered the Gambioni condo in Trump Towers West. Marcus was not severely injured because he was behind Jenna, who shielded him somewhat. Seeing he was suffering severe remorse due to Jenna's condition and the death of his friend, Sal, the CIA sent him on assignment to Europe. It involved working with MI6 on the continent. They felt it would help him clear his mind.

Made in the USA
San Bernardino, CA
24 August 2017